Selected Stories of Rabindranath Tagore

Selected Stories of Rabindranath Tagore

Translated by

Purnima Mazumdar

Ocean Books Pvt. Ltd.

ISO 9001:2015 Publishers

Published by
Ocean Books (P) Ltd.
4/19 Asaf Ali Road,
New Delhi-110 002 (INDIA)
e-mail: info@oceanbooks.in

ISBN 978-81-8430-577-7
SELECTED STORIES OF RABINDRANATH TAGORE
Translated by Purnima Mazumdar

Paperback edition
2020

Price
₹ 150.00 (Rupees One Hundred Fifty only)

Printed at
Narula Printers, Delhi

CONTENTS

1.	Give and Take	7
2.	Postmaster	12
3.	The Return of Khoka Babu	17
4.	The Golden Deer	23
5.	Story at the Riverside	30
6.	Shubha	36
7.	Kabuliwala	43
8.	The Vacation	51
9.	The End—A New Beginning	56
10.	The Last Trophy	69
11.	Rashmoni's Son	71
12.	Taraprasanna's Fame	90
13.	The Hungry Stone	95
14.	Victory and Defeat	102
15.	Charity and Compensation	108
16.	The Editor	113
17.	Elder Sister	116
18.	Grandfather	123
19.	Monihara	130
20.	The Beggar Woman	139

1

GIVE AND TAKE

AT a time when people used to be named after the gods and goddesses, when the little girl was born after five sons, her parents lovingly named her Nirupama. Slowly, Nirupama (Niru) grew up into a beautiful girl. Her parents started searching for a suitable boy for her to marry. Her father, Ram Sunder Mitra, looked everywhere, but was not satisfied with the kind of proposals he was getting. Ultimately, he found a prospective groom for his daughter—the only son of a Rai Bahadur. Although his property and wealth had depleted quite a lot, yet, it was a renowned family. The groom's side asked for Rs 10,000 and all the things required in a household. Without thinking, Ram Sunder agreed to all their conditions—after all, he did not want to lose this prospect.

To meet their demands, he sold off a lot many things, mortgaged some, borrowed from here and there, but all he managed to collect was about Rs 4,000. That left about Rs 6,000 more to be collected. And the day for the wedding was closing in. Someone had promised to give the amount at a very high rate of interest, but, at the time, he was not available. On the day of the wedding, Ram Sunder spoke to Rai Bahadur and pleaded to carry on with the wedding and promised to give rest of the money as soon as possible. There was quite a hullabaloo at the wedding. Then finally, Rai Bahadur said that until he gets the money in hand, the bridegroom shall not sit for the wedding.

There was a hue and cry everywhere, but the bride, sitting

inside, nicely dressed up, trying to calm down the rising question in her mind whether she would be able to devote herself towards her in-laws. Just then the groom, in a manner of disobedience got up and said to his father, "I do not understand all these things about buying and selling, I have come to marry and shall therefore, do the same."

The father was so disappointed at his son's behaviour that he went around telling all and sundry, "See the behaviour of today's youth." Some agreed with him though the marriage, however, took place without any hurdle.

Before going to her in-laws' place, Nirupama hugged her father, who was unable to hold back his tears, and said, "Will they not let me come here again, father?"

"Why won't they?" said Ram Sunder, "I shall bring you."

Ram Sunder often used to go to visit his daughter, but he was not treated well—even the servants would look down upon him. He would generally meet his daughter only for five minutes in the outside room and sometimes, had to come back without meeting her. He could not bear this insult any more, so he decided to pay the money anyhow as he was already shouldering the burden of a lot of credit. He had a tough time making both ends meet. He started avoiding his creditors.

The in-laws, on the other hand, continued to treat his daughter badly and used to pass scornful remarks. As she could not tolerate the criticism of her family, she used to lock herself up in her room and cry her heart out. When someone commented on her beauty, her mother-in-law would say, "She looks as good or bad as her family is."

Probably, the disrespect and insult that the daughter had to suffer, reached the ears of the father. So, Ram Sunder decided to try and sell off the ancestral house. But, it did not strike him then, that he would be depriving his sons of their home. He had decided that he'd sell the house but retain it on rent—in such a manner that his sons would not get to know of the sale before his death; but, the sons came to know about it. They all came and started crying—especially the first three who were married and had children. Their objections and protests became so stern that Ram Sunder postponed the sale of his house and started collecting small sums at high rates.

Niru could understand everything by simply looking at her father's appearance—his hair greyed; his face was shrivelled and showed signs of his poverty and tension. It was difficult for a father to hide his guilt. In order to console her father, Niru longed to go home for a few days. So, one day she told her father to take her away. Ram Sunder agreed but he felt he did not have the right to do so till he had paid the balance amount. Yet, he could not disregard his daughter's request.

So, with a lot of humility, he somehow collected Rs 3,000, tied them up in a handkerchief and went to meet Rai Bahadur. He talked about the weather, gossiped about the neighbourhood and then said, "I know I still have to give you the money. I do pick it up and then, get so involved in some work, that I forget it. After all, I am growing old." So saying, he picked up the notes and put them before Rai Bahadur.

Rai Bahadur only laughed and said, "Relax, I don't need it." After this, no one could talk about the proposal of taking the girl home. Then thinking that this hesitation was not called for, Ram Sunder whispered the request. Without giving any excuses, Rai Bahadur said, "It will not happen now," and walked out. Ram Sunder picked up the sheet in which he had tied the bundle of notes and muttering, that till such time that he is not able to pay the entire amount, he'll not come to this house, he went out.

A number of days passed. Practically everyday, Niru would send one person after another, but her father did not come. Finally, humiliated, she stopped sending people home. This hurt her father, yet, he went.

It was October. Ram Sunder decided that he would definitely get 'The Mother' (goddess) home this time, or else…

On the fifth or the sixth day, Ram Sunder once again tied the notes and proceeded towards his daughter's house. As he was leaving, his 5-year old grandson came and said, "Grandfather, are you going to buy a car for me?" Just then, his 6-year old granddaughter came and said that she did not have any dress fit enough to be worn to a party. All Ram Sunder did was contemplate while chewing tobacco, for he was already aware of all this. He heaved a sigh as he thought of the kind of saris and ordinary jewellery his wife and daughters-in-law would wear if invited to Rai Bahadur's house.

He entered Rai Bahadur's house. Now, he felt a little more confident. He did not have any hesitation. He was told that Rai Bahadur was not at home and that he would have to wait for some time. So, he went to meet his daughter. Tears of joy could not be held back any longer, both the father and the daughter cried. Neither of them could speak. After some time, Ram Sunder said, "I'll take you there this time. Now there's no problem."

Just then, his eldest son suddenly entered with his two sons and said, "Does that mean, father, that now, you have rendered us homeless?" Ram Sunder was stunned. He said, "Will you people not let me do as I please and fulfil my commitments?" He was irritated that despite all his efforts, his sons had come to know that he had sold off the house. His two grandsons clung on to his knees and said, "*Dado* (grandfather), you did not buy me a car." Not getting a reply from their grandfather, the children went to their aunt and said, "*Pishima* (father's sister), will you buy me a car?"

Nirupama understood everything. She said, "*Baba* (father), if you give even a paisa to my father-in-law, then, you'll never again be able to see your daughter, I swear by you."

Ram Sunder said, "Stop it! Don't talk like that. If I can't give this money then it'll be an insult to both—you and your father."

Niru said, "If you give the money, it's an insult! Doesn't your daughter have any prestige? Am I a money bag—that I have value only so long as I have money? No *Baba.* You please do not insult me by giving this money. Besides, my husband has not asked for this money."

"In that case, they won't let you go," said Ram Sunder.

Nirupama said, "What can you do in that case? You also

don't have the permission to take me."

Ram Sunder picked up the roll of money and went back home hesitatingly.

However, the fact that Ram Sunder had brought the money and, at the insistence of his daughter, he had taken it back, could not be kept a secret. The maid told all about it to Niru's mother-in-law. It became a living hell for Nirupama and meeting with any member of her family was banned.

One day, Nirupama suffered an intense pain. Not that her mother-in-law was totally responsible for it, but even Nirupama had stopped caring for her health. She'd go around without warm clothes in winters too and wouldn't eat properly either.

When she became really ill, she told her mother-in-law that she desired to meet her father and her brothers. The mother-in-law reacted by saying that this was only an excuse to go to her father's house. Day-by-day Niru's condition deteriorated. And the doctor came to see her only on the day when she breathed her last.

The eldest daughter-in-law of the house had died. All the rites and rituals were followed—everyone praised them for the way things were done—even sandalwood was used for her cremation. It was difficult to console the father.

However, Rai Bahadur again married off his son and this time demanded Rs 20,000 as dowry.

2

POSTMASTER

WHEN he started his job, the first place he was posted to was Ulapur village. There was a bungalow close by. Using a lot of pull, the *saheb* of that bungalow had got this post office established. The postmaster belonged to Kolkata. Posting him in this village was like pulling a fish out of water and placing it on a boat. His office was in a dark and dingy place with a pond some distance away, around which were dense forests. All the people around were the most ordinary and not fit enough to mix around with the master of the bungalow—especially people from Kolkata. They can't mix very easily. That is why our postmaster could not mix with the local people. There was not too much work either. So, he'd tried his hand at poetry.

He received a very meagre salary. He'd cook for himself. An orphan girl from the village would come and do the other household chores. All she'd receive from him were the four times meal. She was about 12 or 13 years old. There didn't seem much possibility of her getting married. Her name was Ratan.

In the evening, when the drunk *bauls* (traditional singers) would start singing loudly and lamps would be lit, then the postmaster would also light a lamp in his house and call out to Ratan. Ratan would sit outside, waiting for this call, but would not come immediately. Then, she'd come and say, "Say, *dadababu*, why were you calling me?"

Postmaster, "What were you doing?"

Ratan replied, "I was just going to light the fire."

Postmaster said, "That will be done later. Why don't you light my hubble-bubble?"

Without any delay, Ratan would come into the room, hubble-bubble in hand, blowing into the fire. The postmaster would take it and then say, "Alright Ratan, do you ever remember your mother?"

She had a faint memory. However, there were some things that she remembered clearly. One was that her father used to love her more than her mother did. After working hard the whole day long, the father would return home...one or two days were very clearly etched in her mind even today. She remembered how on some rainy days, she and her brother would climb on to broken branches of trees and pretend to be catching fish.

Sometimes it would become very late and the postmaster would not feel like cooking. So, Ratan would quickly make a few rotis and the postmaster would have them with the morning vegetables.

Sometimes, the postmaster used to keep sitting in his office, remembering his family—his mother, younger brother and elder sister. He'd speak about it to this illiterate young girl and it did not seem strange. It became such an everyday thing that the girl started calling his family members *ma, didi, dada* and etched a picture of them in her mind.

One rainy day, on a clear afternoon, a warm breeze was blowing. The postmaster was enjoying the smell of the dry leaves and the monotonous tune of some birds' song. He did not have any work to do. He felt it would have been good if he had someone close with him to share all this.

Heaving a sigh, the postmaster called out to Ratan. Ratan was sitting under the guava tree with legs stretched out before her. She came running and panting and said, "*Dadababu*, what are you thinking about?" The postmaster said, "I shall teach you how to read and write." And, the whole afternoon, he taught her the vowels. In a few days, he succeeded in teaching her a few words.

It was the month of *Shraavan*. There didn't seem to be an end to the rainy season. The drains were overflowing. There was hardly anyone on the roads.

One early morning, it was very cloudy. The postmaster's pupil had been waiting for a long time at the gate, but nobody called out to her. So, she slowly went into the room. She saw that the postmaster was lying on his cot. She thought he was resting, so, she decided to come out. Suddenly, she heard him call out her name in a virtual whisper. Quickly, she went in and said, "*Dadababu*, were you sleeping?" In a troubled voice, the postmaster said, "I don't seem to be feeling well. Just touch my forehead and see if I have fever."

The little girl took on the role of his mother.

She called the *vaidya*, gave the postmaster his medicines on time, sat up all night, cooked for him and asked him a hundred times, "Tell me *Dadababu*, are you feeling a little better?"

After a long time, the postmaster recovered and left his bed. But, he was still very weak. He decided that he would try and get posted out of this place. So, the next day itself, he applied for a posting near Kolkata.

After bringing the postmaster back to health, Ratan, once again, took her place outside the house, but now, no one called out to her as before. She'd often peep inside and see the postmaster either sitting or lying on the cot, deep in thought. For few days Ratan would wait for his call but the postmaster was waiting impatiently for a reply to his application. The girl read her lessons a thousand times, fearing what would happen if he asked her and she was not able to read what he had taught her.

Then, after about a week, the postmaster called out to her. With an anxious heart, the girl entered the room and said, "Did you call me, *Dadababu*?"

The postmaster said, "Yes, Ratan. I am going away tomorrow itself."

Ratan, "Where are you going, *Dadababu*?"

Postmaster, "I am going home."

Ratan, "When will you come again?"

Postmaster, "I won't come now."

Ratan did not ask him anything else. The postmaster himself told her that he had applied for a posting, but it had been rejected. That is why he had resigned from the service and was now, going back home. For long moments, neither of them spoke.

After a while, Ratan got up and slowly walked to the kitchen to make the rotis, but did not do it as fast as on the other days. Probably, she had a lot of tension in her mind. After the postmaster had finished eating his meal, the little girl asked him, "*Dadababu*, will you take me with you to your house?"

The postmaster laughed and said, "How can I do that?" He did not think it necessary to explain the reasons to the little girl. The whole night, the postmaster's laughter and his reply kept ringing in the little girl's mind.

At dawn, when the postmaster woke up, he saw that the water for his bath had been prepared. As had been his habit from Kolkata, he would bathe in stored water. For some reason, the girl had not been able to ask him when he would set out on his journey. So, in the middle of the night itself, Ratan had brought the water from the river. After his bath, the postmaster called out to Ratan. Without a sound, Ratan came to the room and waited patiently for orders from her master. At last, he said, "Ratan, I shall tell the man who is coming to replace me here. He'll be as good to you as I was. You don't have to worry only because I am going away."

For a long time, Ratan had tolerated many of her master's words, but these soft words, she could not bear. She broke down completely and cried, "No...no...you don't have to say anything to anybody. I do not want to stay here." The postmaster had not seen this aspect of Ratan. He was stunned.

The new postmaster arrived. After explaining his charge to him, the old postmaster was about to leave, when he called Ratan and said, "Ratan, I have never been able to give you anything. Now, at the time of my departure, I am giving you something. It'll last for some time."

Leaving aside a little money for his travelling, he took out his salary from his packet. Ratan fell to the ground, held his feet and said, "I beg you *Dadababu*, you don't have to give me anything. I beg you, no one should worry about me." And...she ran out from there.

The ex-postmaster heaved a sigh, slung his bag over his shoulder, took his umbrella and putting his blue and white-striped suitcase on the porter's head, started towards the boat.

When the boat finally started and he heard the sound of the ripples of water beneath, the postmaster felt a pang in his heart. For a moment he longed to return and bring that orphan girl back with him, but then, he realised that there would be many such partings, many such deaths. What will the result of returning be?

Ratan, however, had no such thoughts. She kept going round and round that post office, shedding her tears. She probably had some hope that her *Dadababu* would return. She could not go into the room. O foolish heart! It refuses to believe even the strongest proof.

3

THE RETURN OF KHOKA BABU

I

WHEN Raicharan first came to serve at the house of his masters, he was 12 years old. He belonged to Jessore. He had long hair, big eyes, a slim body, and wheatish complexion. By caste, he was a *Kayastha*. Even his masters were *Kayasthas*. His main work was to protect and help in bringing up the one-year-old child of his master. Ultimately, that child grew taller than Raicharan, finished school, college, and then started working, but Raicharan continued in their service. He now had another one to serve. Now, Anukool *babu* had married and there was a mistress in the house.

The mistress had taken away some of Raicharan's rights, but had given him another right, that of bringing up her newly-born son. Raicharan had, of his own accord, influenced the child so much, that the moment he would see Raicharan, he'd be thrilled. When the child started crawling, he'd come across the threshold and when anyone came to hold him, he'd laugh and quickly try to hide in some safe place...and Raicharan would praise his intelligence and cleverness. He'd go to the mistress and then say, "Your son will become a judge when he grows up. He'll earn Rs 5,000 a month."

Raicharan could not just imagine that any human child could cross the threshold as cleverly as this child could. When the child started toddling, it was amazing! And when he started calling his mother, *Ma*, his aunt, *Pishi* and Raicharan, *Channa*, Raicharan would narrate the incident to all and sundry. Actually it was difficult to say how this distinction enters the mind of a small child. Obviously, no elderly person could teach this to him.

After some time, he'd put a rope around Raicharan's mouth and the latter had to pretend to be his horse. Sometimes, he'd have to pretend to be a wrestler, also pretend to get beaten and fall to the ground.

Just at that time, Anukool *babu* got posted to a district on the banks of the river Padma. Anukool took a cart, a satin shirt, a *zari* embroidered cap and a gold bangle from Kolkata for his son.

Raicharan used to take the boy out for a walk two times a day. It was the rainy season. The Padma river was flooded and slowly, one after another, the gardens and even the villages started getting flooded. It was still cloudy, and there did not seem any possibility of the rain stopping. Raicharan's small master was not willing to stay at home. He went and sat on top of the cart. Raicharan slowly pushed the cart to the banks of the river. There was not a single boat or any human being there. Through a gap in the clouds, he saw that it was the time for the sun to set. In that quietness, the small child raised a finger and shouted, "*Channa, Phoo*."

Raicharan saw a *Kadamb* flower blossom. A few days back, Raicharan had plucked a few of these flowers and made a cart with them, for his *Khoka babu*. The child had probably liked pulling the cart. Raicharan did not have to act as a horse. Now, he did not feel like going over the mud and getting the flowers for the child. So, he immediately pointed in the opposite direction and said, "See…see the bird. It has flown away." He was trying to push the cart away quickly, but it is very difficult to keep away the mind of such a child. There was nothing interesting around.

When the child insisted, Raicharan said, "In that case, you keep sitting in the cart. I'll just run across and get the flower for you. Beware! Don't go near the water!" But, a child is a child. He saw the ripples of water gurgling past him. He longed to touch it. So, he climbed down the boat. He picked up a long straw, pretended it was his fishing rod and started fishing. The naughty waves, in their own language, invited the small boy to come and play in their playroom. There was a 'splash' once, but it obviously could not have been heard very far.

Raicharan had picked a large number of flowers. Smiling, he came to the cart and realised that the child was not there. Raicharan became cold in a second. He gave a loud cry—"*Babu...Khoka babu...*my darling *Dadababu*"—but nobody called back '*Channa*'. There was no sound of any small child—no sound—except that of the river Padma, flowing incessantly, as if it did not know anything and did not have even a minute to wait and think.

As evening had set in, the mistress sent servants in all directions, they saw Raicharan shouting out for the boy like a madman and brought him home. As many times as he was asked, he'd say, "I don't know."

Although everyone understood that it was the doing of Padma, yet even the group of people who had collected in the village suspected Raicharan. The mistress had no doubt that it was he. In fact, she even called him and said, "You bring back my son; I'll give you as much money as you ask for." All Raicharan could do was beat his forehead. And, he was turned out. Anukool *babu* had tried to tell his wife that it was unfair to suspect him, but she did not agree. She said that Raicharan had done so because her son was wearing gold jewellery.

II

Raicharan went back to his village. He did not have any children, nor was there any hope of having any. But, by God's grace, before the end of the year, his wife gave birth to a son. She, however, died in child birth. Raicharan had something against the child. He felt that the child had come to take his *Khoka babu's* place by deceit. He felt that enjoying a son after drowning his master's son, was a crime. Had his widowed sister not been around, Raicharan would probably not have let the child live for long.

What was surprising; however, was that this child, like *Khoka babu*, started crossing the threshold at a very young age. In fact, his behaviour and his voice were also quite similar to his master's son. Sometimes, when the child cried, it seemed as if *Khoka babu* were crying because he had lost Raicharan in his previous birth. At the right time, Phailna—name given by Raicharan's sister—started calling his aunt *Pishi*. Hearing that cry, one day, Raicharan felt that *Khoka babu* had not been able to forget his love for him. That is why he had come to his house as his son. There were many incidents that supported this belief. First, he was born after *Khoka babu's* demise and that too, after his wife had not conceived for so many years. His behaviour was also identical to that of *Khoka babu's*.

Suddenly, Raicharan thought to himself, "That is what a mother's love is. That is why *Khoka babu's* mother had come to know that I had stolen her son." It was then that Raicharan, who had, for so many days, neglected and ignored his son, started feeling guilty. Now, Raicharan started bringing Phailna up as if he were the son of a rich family. He made him wear satin clothes. He melted his dead wife's gold ornaments and got bangles and a necklace made for Phailna. He was not allowed to play or mix around with the children of the neighbourhood. Whenever these children got a chance, they'd tease him by calling him the son of a *nawab*. People were surprised at this behaviour of Raicharan.

When it was time for Phailna to get education, Raicharan sold off all his property and went to Kolkata. He took up a job and sent him to school. He'd give him good clothes, good food and good education. In his heart, he'd say, "Just because you loved me, you came to my house. Do you think you'll not be taken care of because of that? That's not true."

Twelve years passed. The child studied well and was also good to look at—wheatish complexion, and stylish. He never treated his father as his father. That was only because Raicharan had himself kept it a secret from everyone that he was Phailna's father.

Raicharan was growing old. His master always found faults with his work. It was actually because he was physically incapable of handling the job and would forget things. He had now also finished all his money. Phailna had now started complaining about his clothes too.

III

One day, Raicharan resigned from his job and after giving a certain amount of money to Phailna, said, "I have to go to the village for some days on some urgent business." So saying, he went to Barasat. Anukool *babu* was the *moopef* there at that time.

Anukool *babu* did not have another child; his wife was still sorry at the loss of her son.

One day, *babu* was resting after returning from court, while his wife was sitting with a sage, who was giving her some roots so that she would get a son. They suddenly heard the sound of, "May you be victorious!" The master got up and enquired, "Who is it?"

Raicharan entered, saluted and told them who he was. Anukool *babu* was very upset. He felt that Raicharan was responsible for his present condition. Yet, he took him inside to meet his wife, as he had desired. She did not welcome him happily. Not caring for it, Raicharan said, "Master, madam! I only, had stolen your son—neither river Padma, nor anyone else. I am that ungrateful wretch..."

Anukool *babu* said, "What are you saying? Where is he?"

"He is with me. I shall bring him the day after tomorrow," replied Raicharan.

It was Sunday and so, there was no court that day. Both husband and wife were waiting longingly. At 10 a.m., Raicharan walked in with Phailna.

Anukool's wife did not ask Phailna anything. She only pulled him to her, touched him, admired his face, cried, laughed and became hysterical. After all, he was a handsome lad. Although even he was thrilled, yet, Anukool *babu* asked, "What proof do you have?"

Raicharan said, "How can one have proof of such a thing? Only God knows that I had kidnapped your son—nobody else knows anything."

Anukool contemplated; and then decided that his wife had been thrilled at getting her son back. Now, it would be very difficult to take him away from her. So, it was better to believe Raicharan. Besides, where would Raicharan find a son now?

By talking to the boy, he got to know that he had been living with Raicharan since childhood and knew him only as his father.

Getting rid of all doubts, Anukool *babu* said, "But Raicharan, you will not be allowed to stay with us."

Raicharan folded his hands and said, "Where will I go in this old age?"

Anukool *babu's* wife said, "Oh! Let him be. He may bring good luck to my son. I have forgiven him."

Anukool *babu* said, "One cannot forgive what you have done. It is not right to trust a traitor." Raicharan caught his feet and said, "It was not I. It was my destiny. I have no one on this earth."

Phailna was watching all this. He said, "Father, please forgive him. Don't let him stay at home, but fix him a monthly pension."

Raicharan did not say a word. He looked at his son and went out.

At the end of the month, when Anukool *babu* sent some money to Raicharan's village, it came back. There was no man called Raicharan...

4

THE GOLDEN DEER

ADYANATH and Baidyanath Chakravarty were cousins. Of the two of them, the condition of Baidyanath was not so good. His father, Mahesh Chandra, was not very worldly-wise. He was completely dependent on his brother Shivanath, who appeared to be very sweet to his brother, but very cleverly, took away all his property. The only thing Baidyanath got was a few papers of a company.

Shivanath got his son Adyanath married to the only daughter of a very rich man. Mahesh Chandra, on the other hand, got his son Baidyanath married to the eldest daughter of a poor Brahmin without taking even one paisa as dowry. The only reason he probably did not take dowry from the poor Brahmin was that the poor Brahmin had seven daughters and one son. However, Baidyanath helped the poor Brahmin in the marriage of his daughters beyond his means.

After his father's death, Baidyanath was very happy to get the papers and never once thought about doing some work for living. The only work he would do would be to cut the branches of trees and scrape and chisel them so as to make beautiful sticks. Young boys would come to him for these sticks and he would give them in charity. Besides this, a lot of his time would go in making kites. By the grace of God, he had two sons and one daughter.

His wife Mokshada Sundari's dissatisfaction was growing

day by day. She would always compare her house to Adyanath's house. How and why could she not dress up and have all the jewellery that the lady of the house had? And this when both of them belonged to the same family. They had become so prosperous only by depriving them of all their property. The more she would think about it, the more Mokshada would disrespect and hate her father-in-law and his only son. She did not like anything of her house—even the bed seemed worse than a coffin.

Baidyanath would sit outside and keep carving the sticks without uttering a single word—but that was not the solution. Sometimes, the lady of the house would call him inside and looking seriously the other way, would say, "Stop the milkman from giving milk." Irritated, Baidyanath would ask, "How will you manage by stopping the milk? What will the children drink?"

Sometimes, she would show contrary behaviour. She'd call Baidyanath and say, "I don't know how you will do this, but please go and buy the monthly groceries." And, she would give such a long list that could cater to a huge celebration of a prince. If he said, "Why is so much necessary?"; she'd lose her temper and say, "In that case, let the children die of hunger. Let me also go. Then you can stay alone and you can run the household very cheaply."

Baidyanath soon understood that just carving canes would not do. He'd have to do something. Service or business was beyond his means. So, he'd have to discover some new path to *Kuber's* store room.

So one night, while lying restlessly in bed, he prayed, "O Goddess Jagadamba! If only you'd tell me a patent medicine for some incurable disease, I would make a lot of money by telling people about that medicine."

That night, Baidyanath dreamt that his wife was dissatisfied with him and had therefore, pledged her 'remarriage'. Despite his poverty, he dreamt that he was protesting about where he would be able to get so much jewellery from. He knew he had a solid reply for it, but what it was he could not get to his mind. Then, he awoke and saw that it was dawn. He wondered why his wife wanted remarriage. Just then, he realised why he was very upset at the thought.

The next day, after finishing the morning chores, he was sitting and doing some work when a sage entered. Just then, Baidyanath, in the light, saw the idol of his future wealth. They looked after the hermit very well. After a lot of efforts, they came to know that the hermit could make good jewellery, and had no objection in giving him that knowledge.

Even his wife got excited. Just as a jaundice patient sees yellow everywhere, the same way, she also started seeing gold everywhere—the golden bed, the house, etc. and then, in her heart, she invited Goddess Vindhyavasini too. The sage continued staying on and the husband and wife continued serving him. The children did not get their meals on time, they'd fall, get hurt, cry, but neither the husband nor the wife had any regrets. They would continue sitting before the fire, doing the sacrifice. They spent all the money, equivalent to the papers of the two companies. Finally, the sage told them that the gold would appear the next day.

No one slept that night. The husband and wife kept building an illusionary golden city the whole night. There were differences of opinion which led to arguments but because of the joy that they felt, it did not take them long to find a solution.

When the next day dawned, the sage was nowhere to be seen. Forget the gold; even the sunlight was appearing dull. They realised they had lost everything they had. Now, if ever Baidyanath gave any advice regarding the house, the wife would scream, "Had enough of your brain! Now stay quiet for a few days." Baidyanath lost his spirit completely. Mokshada adopted an attitude as if she had, not even for a moment, been convinced or assured and been a part of this plan.

The criminal Baidyanath started thinking of ways to satisfy his wife. In fact, one day, he got a gift secretly for his wife and jokingly said, "Guess what I have brought."

Hiding her curiosity, his wife said, "How can I say?"

Slowly Baidyanath opened the string, then unfolded the

papers carefully and held up a coloured photograph before his wife. She, however, was immediately reminded of the oil painting in her sister-in-law's house. In anger, the wife said, "Wow! Please keep it in your sitting room and keep admiring it."

Baidyanath realised that besides the other qualities, God had also not imparted the knowledge of understanding a woman's mind to him.

Mokshada showed her horoscope and got her palm read by practically all the astrologers she could get in touch with and each one of them said that she'd die before her husband, but that was not the only thing she wanted. She heard that she was lucky as far as children were concerned—but that also didn't please her much. Then, one person told her that if within a year or so, Baidyanath does not acquire some ancestral property, then, burn all his books, etc. Now, Mokshada did not have even an iota of doubt in her mind. The soothsayer went away with a lot of money.

Mokshada would encourage her husband to get a lot of wealth from somewhere, anyhow. Baidyanath felt he could not find any way of getting it. Where should he start digging from, which pond should he dive into or which wall would have to be broken down, he could not decide.

Mokshada was extremely irritated. She told her husband that she did not know that men could be so stupid. She would say, "Hover about. Find out! If you think that money is going to fall from the sky, you are mistaken." It was right and Baidyanath agreed with it too. But which way should he move—no one told him that. So, he again sat outside and started carving canes.

The Durga *puja* celebrations were nearing. On the fourth day of *Ashwin* (September), boats came and touched the harbour. The migrants were returning home. They were carrying yam, coconut, shoes, umbrellas, clothes, books and oil. Wearing a *tussar* Chinacoat, with a stole on his shoulder and an umbrella over his head, a man was going towards a house—Baidyanath was sitting and watching all this and sighing. Subconsciously, he started comparing his house to that of the thousands of Bangladeshis and thought to himself, "Why has the Almighty made me so useless?"

The children had got up early in the morning and were going to Adyanath's courtyard to see the Goddess being made. At lunch time, the maid went and brought them back. Baidyanath was sitting and reminiscing. He pulled the children out of the maid's hands and asked the elder one, "Alright, Abu! What do you want for *puja* this time?"

Immediately Avinash replied, "Will you give me a boat, father?" Even the younger one wanted a boat. The father agreed to give it.

One of Mokshada's uncles also returned to the village at this time. He was an advocate by profession and he had a big house in Kashi. For a few days, Mokshada visited him regularly. Then finally, one day she came to her husband and said, "You'll have to go to Kashi." Baidyanath felt that somehow his wife had got to know that it was time for him to die and that is why she had found this excuse to get rid of him.

Later on, he heard that there was a house in Kashi where there was the likelihood of finding a treasure. Baidyanath said, "O Hell! I will not be able to go to Kashi." Baidyanath had never left home and gone out. Two or three days passed. Baidyanath would sit and carve wood to make the boats. He even made a man rowing the boat and the sail. One could not but appreciate this handiwork. He gave them to his sons. They danced with joy because they had only asked for a boat. This had all the other things too. It seemed so real! Hearing the screams of joy, Mokshada came in, saw the boats, got angry, cried, beat her forehead and then, picked up the two boats and threw them out of the window. The younger son howled loudly. At this, Mokshada gave him a tight slap. The elder son just looked at his father's sad face and became quiet.

Baidyanath agreed to go to Kashi the next day, but where was the money? His wife sold off her jewellery and gave it to him. Baidyanath felt like he was going to die. He called his sons to him and amid tears, kissed them and bade them farewell. Even

Mokshada cried when he was leaving for Kashi.

Baidyanath stayed at his uncle-in-law's house, who was away in the village. So, Baidyanath was staying alone in the house.

One night, he felt a little feverish. So he lit a lamp, kept it by his head, covered himself and went off to sleep. But somehow, he could not sleep. He was suddenly woken up by the tinkling of anklet bells, piercing the quiet of the night. Baidyanath felt frightened, but curiosity got the better of him. He roamed from one room to another to find out who was there, but in vain. In the daytime however, the sound could not be heard.

At midnight, the sound of the tinkling bells was heard yet again. This went on for a number of days. Finally one day, Baidyanath closed all the doors and taking a hammer in his hands, went about tapping all the floors. In one small room close by, he got the sound of emptiness. So at night, he broke the floor. He saw a room below, but decided not to put his foot into it at night. He covered the hole with his bedding and slept. But the sound had become so loud and clear now, that he quickly got up from there and came away. But, he could not get himself to leave the house unprotected and go away. Fear and greed—both held him back.

The next morning, the same sound was heard. Baidyanath sat outside only. Then, he went inside and locked the door. Then taking God's name, he removed his bedding from over the hole. He could hear the sound of water and the falling of coins very clearly. Slowly, he brought his face close to the hole and peeped in. He saw water coming out from the centre of the room—but he could not see much in the darkness. He put a long rod and saw that it was only knee deep. He took a kerosene lamp and a match box and jumped into it suddenly. He saw a copper pitcher tied with a thick iron chain. When the flow of the water was heavy, it would push the chain against the pitcher. That would make a sound. He waded his way through the water and went close to the pitcher. He was disappointed to see that the pitcher was empty. He could not believe his eyes. He turned the pitcher this way and that, but in vain. Disappointed, Baidyanath put both his hands into the water and started searching for something like a madman.

Suddenly his hand hit against something. He picked it up. It was the head of a skeleton. He shook even that to see if there was something inside it. Finding nothing, he threw it away.

Then, he noticed that the wall towards the river was broken, but there was nothing there either. Finally, disappointed, he came out, covered with mud. He dreaded the fact that he would, once again, have to pack his belongings and return to argue with his wife.

His uncle-in-law, on returning from the village, became very angry at his foolish act. He advised him to return to the village. He returned one winter evening. He had watched migrants returning home, but had never imagined he would do the same some day. On reaching home, he sat outside his house only and did not go in. Then, the maid saw him and shouting in joy, announced his homecoming. His sons came running and his wife called him in. He took one child in his arms and holding the other child's hand, went in.

A lamp was burning in a corner. For some time, Baidyanath stood quietly, and then asked his wife how she had been. Without giving any answer, his wife asked him what had happened. Without giving any reply, Baidyanath only slapped his forehead. Mokshada looked at him sternly. The children guessed that something was wrong, so they slowly walked out from there and asked the maid to tell them a story.

For some time Mokshada and Baidyanath sat quietly, staring at each other. Then, Mokshada entered her room and bolted it from inside. Baidyanath kept standing outside, quietly. At about midnight, his elder son came to the verandah and called out his father, but he was not there. Frightened, he returned and lay down in bed.

In the morning the maid prepared Baidyanath's hubble-bubble and went looking for him, but could not find him anywhere. The neighbours came—but they too, could not find him anywhere.

5

STORY AT THE RIVERSIDE

IF one could carve incidents on stone, there would be innumerable tales on river shores. If anybody wishes to hear of the bygone days, he should sit at the shore and listen quietly to the sound of the whispering water.

It was the month of *Ashwin.* The river was in full flood; only four or five of its steps on the bark were visible—the rest were covered by water. It had crept up to the low—lying parts of the bank, where plants grew densely beneath the branches of the mango tree. Old brick heaps towered above the water where the river bent. The boats of the fishermen had been tied to the trees on the bank, but they could not stay still. They seemed to be floating up and down—being pushed by the tide of the river. The small boats set sail. They seemed like small birds. The sunrays falling on the river seemed golden.

The Brahmin priest, Bhattacharya, came down daily with his sacred vessels, to bathe. The women arrived in groups to fetch water. But it was Kusum whom the river liked very much. Whenever the river saw her reflection in the water, it wanted to hold it! When she used to lay her foot on the river's rock, the bells on her anklet would ring. Not that she used to play a lot or laugh or joke about. But she had the largest number of friends. The river would sometimes, see her sitting near the riverside. She loved water. The river knew this was the time of Kusum's coming to the bathing steps.

After a few days, the river did not see Kusum. Her friends Rekha and Subarna used to come to the banks and cry. They talked sadly as their friend, Kusum, had been taken away to her husband's house—a place where there was no Ganges. It was a strange place with strange people, strange houses and strange roads. It was like pulling a lotus out of water and transplanting it elsewhere.

As time went by, the river almost forgot Kusum. It had been a year. The women rarely spoke of Kusum now. But, one evening, the river was startled by the touch of familiar long-known feet. Ah yes! But those feet were without anklets now. They had lost their old music.

Kusum had become a widow. The river heard that her husband used to work in some far-off place and that she had not met her husband more than once or twice. A letter had brought the news of his death. She had been widowed at the young age of 12 years, the vermilion on her forehead had been wiped off, the jewellery had been taken off and she had come back to her old home by the Ganges. But not many of her friends were left. Rekha, Subarna and Amala had already been married; only Sharat remained but it was said that she too would be married by *Agrahayan*. Kusum was all alone. When she used to sit on the river steps, with her head resting on her folded knees, the river felt like playing with her with its waves.

As the Ganges quickly grows to fullness at the beginning of the rains (monsoon), similarly Kusum too, grew to fullness of beauty and youth day by day. But, her dull coloured sari, her gentle, thoughtful face and quiet manners drew a veil over her youth and hid it from people's eyes. Ten years passed and no one seemed to have noticed that Kusum had grown up. The river too, never thought her to be a young maiden. The river always pictured her as a young girl. Although she did not wear anklets any more, yet the river could hear the sound of her anklets as she walked.

One morning, in late September, a tall, young, fair-complexioned *sanyasi* took shelter in the Shiva temple at the bank of the river. The news of his arrival soon spread throughout the village. The women left their water pots and crowded into the temple to bow to the holy man. The crowd kept on increasing every day. A good-looking sage was the centre of attraction among the girls and women. Besides, he did not disrespect or ignore anyone. He would make the children sit on his lap and would ask the women about their families. The sanyasi's fame spread quickly among the women. Some came to him for advice, some for comfort and some for medicine. The girls would come to the river banks and discuss, "How handsome he is! It seems as if *Mahadeva* has taken the form of a human and come and sat in this temple."

Many more months passed by. In the month of *Chaitra*, at the time of the solar eclipse, huge crowds come here to bathe in the Ganges. Many of the believers went to visit the *sanyasi*. Among them was a party of women from the village where Kusum had been married.

The *sanyasi* was sitting on the river's steps and chanting mantras, when a woman saw him and, nudging her friend, said, "Why! He is our Kusum's husband!" Another parted her veil and shouted, "So he is! He is the younger son of the Chatterjee family of our village!" A third said, "He has exactly the same forehead, nose and eyes!" But, another woman, without turning to the *sanyasi*, dipped her pot into the water and said, "That young man is dead. He will not come back again to Kusum."

Then the others joined the argument, saying, "He did not have such a long beard, he was not so thin" or "I do not think he was so tall." That settled the question for the time being and the matter spread no further. Everyone in the village had seen the *sanyasi* except Kusum. Because a large number of people had collected there, Kusum had stopped coming to the river steps completely.

One evening, as the full moon rose, Kusum came and sat upon my last step above the water. There was no one else at the bathing place. Insects were humming. The ringing of the temple bells had just ended. The soft moonlight shone on the dark waters of the Ganges.

Slowly, the *sanyasi* came out from the temple. Coming down the steps of the bathing place, he saw a woman sitting alone and was turning to go back when suddenly, Kusum raised her head and looked behind her. Her veil slipped away and the moon lighted up her face as she looked up. She looked familiar. An owl flew away over their heads, giving its strange, sad cry. Disturbed by the sound, Kusum quickly put the veil back on her head and bowed low at the sanyasi's feet.

He have her his blessings and said, "Who are you?"

She replied, "My name is Kusum."

No one spoke another word that night. Kusum's house was close by. Slowly, she went back home. But the *sanyasi* kept sitting on the river steps for a long time that night. At last, when the moon passed from east to the west, and the sanyasi's shadow, moving from behind, fell in front of him, he rose and entered the temple.

After this, the river noticed that Kusum came every day to bow at the sanyasi's feet. When he preached, she would stand in a corner and listen to him. After he finished preaching, he used to call her and tell her about religion. She, obviously, could not understand everything, but she listened in silence and tried to understand it. She carefully obeyed all his orders. She served daily at the temple, respectfully worshipping the god; picking flowers for the *puja* and fetching water from the Ganges to wash the temple floor.

All the things that the *sanyasi* told her, she would sit and contemplate on while sitting on the river steps. Slowly, it brought about a change in her. Instead of looking depressed all the time, she had started looking happy and cheerful.

Winter was nearing its end. Now in the evening, a warm spring breeze would blow unexpectedly from the south. The music was heard, once again, in the village, after the long silence of winter. The boatmen set their boats floating down the river and began singing the songs of Krishna.

The river was not able to see Kusum now, so it began to miss her. For some time now, she had given up visiting the temple, the bathing place and the *sanyasi*. The river did not know what happened in between. After some time, one evening, the two of them met on the river steps.

Kusum bowed her head and said humbly, "Master, did you send for me?"

"Yes," answered the *sanyasi*. "Why do I not see you? Why have you started neglecting your duties towards God?" the *sanyasi* asked. But, Kusum kept silent.

"Please tell me what is in your mind," he said gently. Turning her face away, Kusum said, "I have been wicked, master! I have committed a sin. That is why I have failed in my duties."

The *sanyasi* said affectionately, "Kusum, I know that your heart is in turmoil. I understand it."

She gave him a despairing, startled look. She probably felt worried about how much he understood. Tears welled up in her eyes. She sat down there only. Then, pulling her sari over her face, she fell at the sanyasi's feet and wept. The *sanyasi* moved a little away and said, "Please tell me everything about the problem that is there in your heart. Tell me and I will show you the path to peace."

In a voice filled with complete faith, Kusum replied, "I must speak out what is in my heart only because you order it. However, I shall not be able to explain it clearly. You, master, must have known it all. I have worshipped someone as a god and the joy of that perfect love filled my heart. But, one night, I dreamt that the lord of my heart was sitting in a garden somewhere, holding my right hand in his left and whispering to me of love. The whole incident did not seem at all strange or impossible to me. The dream ended but its memory, its impact remained. The next day, when I saw him, I did not see him as before. The dream picture was in my mind. I no longer thought of him as a god but as a man. In fear, I ran away from him but that picture continued to remain with me. Since that day, my heart has known no peace. Everything within me has grown dark."

When Kusum was narrating all this and wiping her tears, the river felt that the *sanyasi* was pressing the stone under his right foot with great force.

When she had stopped crying and finished her story, the *sanyasi* said, "You will have to tell me who you saw in your dreams."

With folded hands, Kusum cried, "Master, I cannot do that." The *sanyasi* insisted, "I am asking you for your good only. Tell me clearly who it was."

Crying, Kusum said, "Master, it was you!" The moment after saying this, she fell down, unconscious. The *sanyasi* stood like a statue.

When she gained consciousness, she sat up, the *sanyasi* said slowly, "You have followed each and everything that I said. I shall tell you one more thing. You'll have to follow it. I am leaving this place tonight itself. You will have to forget me. You must know that I am a *sanyasi* and do not belong to this world."

Kusum got up, looked into his face and, in a low voice, said, "It shall be so, master."

The *sanyasi* said, "I am going now. Goodbye." Without a word, Kusum bowed to him and placed the dust of his feet on her head. And, she murmured, "He has ordered that I must forget him." Then she slowly climbed down into the river. The river heard the sound of something falling into the water. The wind cried madly in the darkness as if it wanted to blow out every star in the sky.

The one who used to play in the river lap, had got lost, the river didn't know where.

6

SHUBHA

AT the time when the girl was named Subhashini (the soft spoken), who would have guessed that she would never be able to speak? Who knew that she would grow up to be a dumb? A mute?

Sukeshini (the one with beautiful hair) and Suhasini (the one with a beautiful smile) were the two sisters of Subhashini (Shubha). As per the custom the two elder sisters had been married off and a lot of money had been spent on their weddings but now, the youngest one lay like a liability on her parents. Even in her presence people used to show their concern about her future. She had understood, from her earliest childhood that God had sent her to her father's house like a curse. So, she kept away from ordinary people and tried to live apart. She felt that she could endure her happiness if everyone would forget her. But, can anyone ever forget pain? Night and day, her parents' mind ached with anxiety on her account—especially her mother, because a mother considers her daughter to be a reflection of her own image.

Banikanta, Shubha's father, loved this silent child of his a little more than his other daughters but her mother felt a sense of shame and almost hated Shubha because she was not like the other girls.

Shubha lacked speech but she had two large, dark eyes and her lips trembled like a leaf in answer to any thought that arose

willingly. She asked Phatik, "What do you say? Will you go to Kolkata with *mama*?" Phatik jumped with joy and said, "Yes."

Although Phatik's mother had no problem bidding him goodbye because she was scared he might hit Makhan some day and break his skull yet she was a little upset at seeing him so keen to go.

"When will we go?" Phatik kept troubling his uncle. He had even lost his sleep in his excitement. Finally, for the joy of travelling, he handed over all his belongings to his younger brother.

When they reached Kolkata, the first person he was introduced to was his aunt who was not really satisfied with this new addition to the family. She already had three sons and now another thirteen year-old, illiterate village boy had been brought in. She was amazed at Vishwambar's stupidness! Didn't he realise that there is no bigger problem in this world than bringing up a teenaged-boy? He was neither good looking nor could he do any work.

Even Phatik knew that he could not adjust here. That is why he was always very apologetic. If he could only be close to some affectionate person, then he would continue having self-respect. No one dared show affection to him. He was like a dog that had lost its master. Hence, any other place except his mother's house was like hell. If only his aunt could give him some work to do, he would have gladly done more than was needed.

He was caught here. So, he would often remember his house in the village. He missed his kite flying, the river, his swimming, his friends and more than that, his unjust mother. There was no other student like him in the whole school. When the teacher asked him any question, he would keep staring with his mouth wide open. He would stand like an ass and patiently take the beating that the master gave him. When the other children played, he'd stand and keep looking at the terraces of the houses.

One day, after making a lot of promises and collecting a lot of courage, he had asked his uncle, "When will we go to mother?" and the uncle had said, "Let the school break for the vacations." The *puja* vacations were still very far.

One day, Phatik lost his books. As it is, he had not prepared his lessons very easily and then, losing the books! The teacher started insulting and hitting him every day. It became so bad that his cousins started feeling ashamed to say that he was related to them. In fact, they even started enjoying his insults.

Feeling helpless, Phatik went to his aunt one day and apologetically, said, "I have lost my books."

His aunt showed disgust and said, "Very well done! I cannot buy the books for you five times a month." Without uttering a word, Phatik came away from there. The thought that he was wasting someone else's money, irritated him so much that he was very angry with his mother. He felt really low.

That night, after returning from school, he felt feverish and complained of a headache. He realised that if he complained, his aunt would say it was only to trouble her. When unwell, the only person this innocent child could expect looking after from, was his mother.

The next morning, Phatik could not be seen anywhere—not in the neighbourhood nor in the houses of friends. That night, it rained heavily. People who were looking for him got completely drenched. Finally, Vishwambar Babu lodged a complaint with the police.

In the evening, a car came and stopped in front of Vishwambar Babu's house. There was knee-deep water. Two policemen brought Phatik out of the car and took him to Vishwambar. His head was wet, his whole body covered in mud, his face and his eyes, bloody red and he was shivering. Vishwambar Babu practically picked him up and took him inside. The moment his aunt saw him, she said, "Why do we have to suffer so for another's son? Send him home." Because of the worry for the boy, she had not dressed or eaten well and had been having arguments with her sons.

Phatik broke down and weeping bitterly, said, "I was going to my mother. They brought me back." His temperature was running very high. He muttered the whole night. Vishwambar Babu came in with a doctor. Phatik opened his eyes once and staring at the ceiling, said, "Uncle, have my vacations begun?" Vishwambar wiped his eyes and holding Phatik's hands, came and sat beside him.

Once again, Phatik started muttering, "Mother, don't hit me. I promise I have not committed any mistake."

The next day, he was conscious for a while. He kept staring at the room, expecting to find somebody. Then, disappointed, he lay down, facing the wall. Vishwambar Babu understood what he wanted. So, lowering his face, he whispered, "Phatik, I have sent for your mother." The doctor came and said that his condition was serious. Vishwambar Babu also waited for the patient's mother.

Just then, Phatik's mother stormed in. Vishwambar made her sit down. She started lamenting loudly, "My Phatik, my beloved!" Phatik just turned on his side and without aiming at anyone, said in a very soft voice, "Mother, my vacations have started. I am going home now."

9

THE END—A NEW BEGINNING

I

AFTER passing his M.A., Apoorva Krishna was returning home from Kolkata. The river usually practically dries up in the summer but now, after heavy rains, it is flooded with water.

The boat in which Apoorva Krishna had come, lay at achor in the harbour. He could see the terrace of his house through the trees. No one knew that he was coming. That is why there was none to receive him. He took his bag from the boatman and hurriedly got off the boat. The ground was slippery. So, the moment he got off, his foot slipped and he fell in the muck. The moment he fell down, he heard a loud, tingling laughter from somewhere.

Embarrassed, Apoorva looked up to see a girl sitting on top of the moneylender's boat, laughing. Apoorva recognised the girl. She was their new neighbour's daughter, Mrinmoyee. Their house was a little far away, across the river, but for the last two or three years, they had been living here.

A number of notorious tales about this girl could be heard. The village men used to affectionately call her *pagli* (mad girl) and the women of the village were always scared, worried, suspicious and apprehensive about her. All the boys of the village were her playmates. She hated the girls of her age. She was the apple of her father's eyes. In fact, Mrinmoyee's mother always used to complain against her to her husband but Mrinmoyee's tears used to upset her father. So her mother could never scold her when her father was around.

Mrinmoyee had a dusky complexion. Her hair was curly and long—it came up to her waist. She had an extremely childlike, innocent face. There was no embarrassment and no fear in those two large eyes. No one ever thought of how old she was because if they had, then they would have stopped criticising her parents. The day the zamindar's boat used to lie at anchor in the harbour here, the girls used to take cover from boat, Mrinmoyee, with a naked child in her arms, her curly hair falling on her back, came and stood there. She kept watching and then, returning to her friends, started discussing about the newcomer.

Apoorva had come during the vacations and had seen this girl twice or thrice and had, during his free time—and also in his busy time—thought about her. There are many faces in this world which attract us but sometimes, there is a face that settles down in our minds—not just for its beauty but for its clarity.

This girl had that naughtiness—that is why one could not forget her face easily.

II

Apoorva finally reached home. His widowed mother was thrilled to see him. She prepared all the things he loved—*kheer, rohu* fish, etc. After the meal, his mother began to talk about his wedding. He was prepared for it. Actually, the proposal had been made earlier only, but he was determined not to marry till he had passed his B.A. He told his mother, "Look for a bride first, then I'll decide." Mother said, "We have already found the girl. You needn't worry about it." Apoorva said, "I will not be able to marry the girl without seeing her." Although his mother did not approve of it, she consented to it.

That night, after he had put off the lights, the sound of loud laughter came in his thoughts. He wanted to convince himself that the girl probably did not know who he was or how qualified he was; that despite the fact that he had fallen down in the mud, he was not the kind who could be laughed at.

The next day, Apoorva was to go and see the girl—not far but in the neighbourhood. He dressed up a little carefully. Instead of the *dhoti*, he wore a silken long coat, a rounded *pugree*, polished shoes and carried a silk umbrella when he went out of the house in the morning.

When he entered the would-be father-in-law's house, it was already time for the celebrations. The girl was dressed, bejewelled, made up and brought before the prospective groom. She was made to sit in a corner with her head bowed down to her knee. There was a maid sitting behind her, trying to prompt and encourage her to answer. A brother of the bride-to-be, continued to inspect or examine the new entrant, the prospective groom's watch, *pugree*, umbrella and chain. Ultimately, stroking his moustache, Apoorva courageously asked, "What do you study?" No answer. After being asked a number of times, when the girl did not answer, the old maid coaxed her. At this, in one breath, she answered, "Charupath Part II; Essence of German Part I; Geography; Mathematics; History of India."

Just then, a loud and fast thumping of feet could be heard and before long, Mrinmoyee ran in panting, with her hair falling all over her back. Without even throwing a glance at Apoorva, she just held the hand of the girl's brother, Raakhaal and started pulling him but he somehow did not want to get up. The maid started cursing Mrinmoyee. Finally, Mrinmoyee gave her friend Raakhaal a box on his back and pulling the veil off the girl's face, ran out like a tornado. Raakhaal burst out laughing. He had quite forgotten the box on his back as it was a very common thing between them. Apoorva also got up to go. When he went near the door, he saw that his polished shoes were not there. Everyone was embarrassed as to where his shoes had disappeared. Finally, he wore the loose, old shoes of the head of the family and returned home.

On the banks of the Pushkarini, he suddenly heard that loud laugh—as if nature was laughing at his state. Then suddenly, a girl came before him, put his new shoes down and was just turning to go when Apoorva held her captive with his hands. Mrinmoyee tried to release herself, but could not. Apoorva looked into her eyes and slowly released his grip. Had he given her a slap also, Mrinmoyee would not have minded it or been surprised. But, this behaviour amazed her. Apoorva came back home slowly.

III

The whole day, Apoorva made innumerable excuses for not going and seeing his mother. Why would a serious person like Apoorva long to tell an uneducated girl all about himself? How does it matter if a village belle considered him to be an ordinary person? Or that she ignored him completely and got all worked up about playing with a boy called Raakhaal? But, it is very difficult to convince oneself and he was not willing to bow down before this naughty girl.

In the evening, as he entered, his mother asked him, "How did you find the girl, Apu? Did you like her?" Apoorva said, "I have seen the girls, mother, and have liked one." Mother was surprised. She said, "How many girls did you see?" After a lot of beating about the bush, it came to light that her son had liked Mrinmoyee. After getting so much of education, is this what his taste was like?

Earlier, Apoorva was a little embarrassed but when mother continued objecting to it, he became adamant and said, "I shall not marry anyone else except Mrinmoyee." After two or three days of hunger strike and sleepless nights, Apoorva finally came out victorious. His mother tried to convince herself that Mrinmoyee was childish and immature and that her mother had failed to give her the right kind of education; that once she gets married and comes under her wings her nature would change. In fact, she even convinced herself that Mrinmoyee had a very pleasant face. But, she would often be reminded of her unkempt hair and she'd feel disappointed. However, she decided that once she comes into her family, she'd oil and comb her hair tightly. Many people of the neighbourhood liked Mrinmoyee but no one ever thought of getting her as a daughter-in-law.

At the right time, the proposal was sent to Mrinmoyee's

father, Ishaan Majumdar. He was working in some shipping company and was posted in some small place near the river. He used to live in a small house with a tin roof. When he heard of the proposal, he could not believe his luck. Anyway, he sent a leave application to the Head Office, but the boss thought that it was too small a thing to go on leave for. So, it was rejected. He wrote back to say that he'd get leave in autumn. So, he'd be happy if the wedding could be postponed till Durga *puja*. But, Apoorva's mother said, "There is an auspicious date this month only. I can not postpone it any more."

So, all the elderly people of the village and her mother started preaching Mrinmoyee day in, day out about how to behave. She was told not to walk so fast, not to talk or laugh loudly, to dress properly and not to play with the boys of the village. Mrinmoyee started feeling as if she was being prepared for the hanging or for the life imprisonment! So, she proclaimed, "I shall not get married." But, she had to get married, like everybody else.

IV

After that, her education started. In just one night, Mrinmoyee's entire world changed on coming into the house of Apoorva's mother. Her mother-in-law started correcting her. Making a stern face, she said, "Look here, little one! You are no longer a small child. Your behaving in this shameless way is not going to work in our house." Mrinmoyee misunderstood what her mother-in-law had said. She felt that she'd have to go elsewhere to do what she wanted to do. So, she went out and could not be seen anywhere. Everyone started looking for her. Finally, the traitor Raakhaal brought her out from her secret place. Her mother-in-law abused her a lot.

At night, it started raining. Apoorva slowly came close to Mrinmoyee and whispered into her ear, "Don't you love me, Mrinmoyee?" Loudly and angrily, Mrinmoyee said, "No. I shall never love you." Hurt, Apoorva said, "Why? What harm have I done you?" Mrinmoyee said, "Why did you marry me?" It is difficult to give a satisfactory reason for this. Apoorva decided that in whatever way he could, he would have to keep his mind under control.

The next day, seeing signs of Mrinmoyee's rebellious nature, her mother-in-law locked her up in a room. Like a newly-caged bird, she first kept throwing things around, then, seeing no way of escaping, she tore the bed sheet into pieces. Then she fell to the floor and amidst tears, continued calling out to her father.

Then she felt that someone had come and sat down beside her. It was Apoorva. He tried to, lovingly, push her hair back, but Mrinmoyee pushed his hand away. Apoorva whispered in her ears, "I have opened the door secretly. Come, let us run away." Loudly, Mrinmoyee said, "No." He tried to raise her head and say, "Look who's come. Raakhaal has come to play with you. Will you go to play?" "No." Raakhaal understood that it was no good. So, he went out. Mrinmoyee went off to sleep, crying and Apoorva came out of the room.

The next day, Mrinmoyee received a letter from her father. Mrinmoyee went to her mother-in-law and said, "I will go to my father." Her mother-in-law got angry and said, "God knows where her father lives and she says 'I'll go to my father!'. Useless request." And, without answering, she went away. Mrinmoyee went into her room and kept saying, "Father, take me away from here. There's no one here for me. I shall not live if I stay here."

In the middle of the night, when her husband was fast asleep, Mrinmoyee opened the door quietly and went out. She did not know the way to her father's house. All she knew was that the postman came from there. It was nearly dawn when Mrinmoyee, passing through the jungles, reached a market place near the sea. She was just contemplating which way to go when she heard a familiar sound. A postman, who was passing that way, came and stood near her. Mrinmoyee immediately went to him and pleaded, "I want to go to my father in Kushiganj. Please take me with you." He said, "I don't know where Kushiganj is." Then, he sat in a boat and started off. He did not have any time to listen to her tales.

Mrinmoyee came to the banks and called a boatman and said, "O boatman! Will you take me to Kushiganj?" Before that boatman could give a reply, someone from a boat harboured close by, said, "Who's that? Minu? How are you here?" Excited at recognising him, Mrinmoyee said, "Banamali, I want to go to meet my father in Kushiganj. Please take me in your boat." It was a boatman from her village. He recognised the girl very well. He said, "You'll go to your father? That's good. Come, I'll take you there." Mrinmoyee climbed on to his boat.

The boat started. So did the rain. As the boat moved on the tide, Mrinmoyee started feeling sleepy and dozed off like a small child. When she awoke, she saw that she was sleeping on her bed in her in-law's house. Seeing her awake, the maid started abusing her. So did her mother-in-law. Mrinmoyee kept staring aghast. However, when the mother-in-law started commenting about her father and the kind of education he had given her, Mrinmoyee stormed out of the room, went into the other room and locked herself from inside. Apoorva came to his mother and said, "What is the harm in sending the girl to see her father for a day or two?" Mother started abusing him also and said that she wondered why he had chosen Mrinmoyee amongst hundreds of girls in the village.

V

Few days passed, Mrinmoyee was very unhappy at her state of affairs. But one day, at midnight, Apoorva woke Mrinmoyee up softly and said, "Do you want to go to your father?" She sat up with a start and holding Apoorva's hands said, "Yes."

Apoorva said, "In that case, come. Let us both escape quietly. I have already fixed up a boat." Full of gratitude, Mrinmoyee looked at her husband lovingly. Then she got up, quickly changed her clothes and came out. So that mother would not worry, Apoorva left a note for her.

That was the first time Mrinmoyee, of her own wish, held her husband's hand and came out in the dark of the night. The boat left the same night. There were many new things that Mrinmoyee could see on both sides of the river and she questioned her husband about each one of them. Apoorva answered each question—whether he knew the answer or not.

The next day, the boat reached Kushiganj. In a tin house, Ishaan Chandra was sitting and writing something in a leather ledger, when the newly-wedded couple entered. Mrinmoyee called out, "Father!" Tears started falling from the eyes of Ishaan. He could not decide what to say or do. His daughter and his son-in-law were like a prince and princess. He could not decide how to make a befitting seat for them. He did not know what to give them to eat. Mrinmoyee said, "We'll all cook together, father." Apoorva showed great excitement at this proposal.

There was a shortage of space, food and help and yet there was happiness all around. Three days went by. Both—morning and evening—the steamer would lie at anchor in the harbour. Innumerable people would come. There'd be loud noises and then it would be quiet. At night there was such freedom! The three of them would cook together—try to prepare something and land up preparing some other dish. Then Mrinmoyee would serve the food. They would eat and criticise her and she would feign anger. Finally, Apoorva said that it would not be right to stay on any longer.

On the day she was leaving, Ishaan Majumdar pulled Mrinmoyee to him and putting his hand on her head, said, "Stay like a good girl in your in-laws' house. Let no one find any fault in my Mrinmoyee."

Crying, Mrinmoyee took leave of her father.

VI

When the defaulter couple came home, Apoorva's mother remained very serious. She did not say anything. She continued showing her silent anger. Ultimately, Apoorva came and said, "Mother, college has reopened. I shall have to go to study Law." Mother said, "What are you going to do about daughter-in-law?" Apoorva said, "She'll stay here only."

Mother said, 'No, no. There's no work here. Take her with you." Preparations started being made for his going to Kolkata. The night before his departure, when he came into his room, he saw Mrinmoyee sitting on the bed and weeping. He was upset. He said, "Don't you want to go with me to Kolkata?"

Mrinmoyee said, "No."

Apoorva asked, "Don't you love me?" He got no reply to this question. He asked, "Are you feeling bad about having to leave Raakhaal and going?" Suddenly, Mrinmoyee said, "Yes." Apoorva said, "I shall not be able to come for a very long time." Mrinmoyee had nothing to say. "It may be two years or more," Apoorva added.

Mrinmoyee said, "When you come, please bring a Swiss penknife for Raakhaal."

"In that case, does that mean that you will stay here only?" asked Apoorva.

Mrinmoyee said, "Yes, I'll stay with mother."

Heaving a sigh, Apoorva said, "Alright, so be it. I shall not come back till such time that you write and call me. Are you happy now?" Not thinking it necessary to answer this question, Mrinmoyee went off to sleep, but Apoorva could not sleep. He kept staring at sleeping Mrinmoyee's face. She looked like a princess who had been magically put to sleep by a wand. All he wanted was a golden wand to awaken her. Early in the morning, Apoorva woke her up and said, "Mrinmoyee, it's time for me to go. Come, I'll leave you at your mother's house."

Just as Mrinmoyee got up, Apoorva held both her hands and said, "Now, I have a request. I have helped you many times. Now, at the time of my departure, will you give me a reward for it?"

Surprised, Mrinmoyee said, "What?"

Apoorva said, "Of your own accord, lovingly, give me a kiss."

Hearing this strange request and seeing Apoorva's serious face, Mrinmoyee burst out laughing. She controlled her laughter, then putting her face forward, went ahead to kiss him—then, she went close and could not control herself—she burst out laughing once again. She tried two more times but finally, just put a cloth to her face and continued laughing. Pretending to discipline her, Apoorva held her by the ears and lovingly, shook her head. Apoorva did not want to force anything out of her. All he wanted was a little gift of love from her.

Apoorva dropped her at her mother's home, came home and told his mother, "After a lot of contemplation, I realised that if I take my wife with me, it'll hamper my studies, and she too will not have any friends. You don't want to keep her in this house and that is why I left her at her mother's home."

The mother and son parted amidst anger and disappointment.

VII

In her mother's house also, Mrinmoyee realised that she did not feel comfortable or at peace. As if everything here had changed. Time just did not seem to pass. She felt as if there was no one in the house or in the entire village; as if the sun had set in the middle of the day. She could not understand why she longed to go to Kolkata today. Where was this desire last night? Last night also, she did not know that the part of her life that she had longed for had changed completely. She never realised when God had brought about a difference between her childhood and her youth. Today, when shaken up, her childhood had been separated from her youth and had fallen and Mrinmoyee had been amazed at her own hurt.

Even her own bedroom in her mother's house seemed strange. All her memories now revolved around that house, that room and that bed that had belonged to her husband.

No one ever saw Mrinmoyee outside the house or heard her laughter. Raakhaal now felt scared to see her and did not even think about playing. Finally, one day, she told her mother, "Please take me to my in-laws' house. Apoorva's mother too, had been very upset at the fact that he had left her daughter-in-law in her mother's house."

One day, with her head covered, Mrinmoyee came and fell at her mother-in-law's feet. With tears in her eyes, her mother-in-law embraced Mrinmoyee. The mother-in-law looked amazed at her daughter-in-law. It was not the same Mrinmoyee. Such a drastic change in the spoilt girl!

Her mother-in-law had thought that she would correct all Mrinmoyee's faults but someone invisible had created such circumstances that Mrinmoyee seemed to have taken a new birth. Now, she had started feeling the pangs of love and had started missing her husband. In her heart, she said, "I did not understand myself; but then why did you not understand me? Why did you not punish me? When I refused to go to Kolkata with you, why did you not take me with you forcibly? Why did you listen to me? Why did you fulfil my request?"

Mrinmoyee remembered each incident—when he had requested her for a kiss! Apoorva, on the other hand, regretted that Mrinmoyee had not recognised him fully. He had told Mrinmoyee that he would not come back until she wrote to him and called him. So one day, Mrinmoyee locked her room and sat down to write a letter. She took out the gold-bordered-letter-writing-paper which he had given her, and started writing. The letters were of different sizes, and the line too, was not straight. Without addressing him, she wrote, "Why did you not write to me? How are you? Come home."

She did not know what else to write. Then, she added, "Now, you write to me and write how you are. Mother is well, so are Bishu and Poonti. Yesterday, our cow Kalo gave birth to a calf." And, she ended the letter. She folded it, put it in an envelope and put down Apoorva's name. She did not know that one had to write the address too. So that her mother-in-law would not see the letter, she gave it to her trusted maid. But, the letter did not yield any result—Apoorva did not come home.

VIII

Mother noticed that despite the fact that the vacations had begun, Apoorva had not come home. She felt that he was still angry with her. So did Mrinmoyee. Time and again, she'd ask the maid, "Did you post the letter?" Answering her for the thousandth time, the maid said, "Yes, I posted it with my own hands. Sir must have got it a long time back."

Finally, one day, Apoorva's mother called Mrinmoyee and said, "Apu has not come home for a long time. Hence I am planning to go to Kolkata to see him. Will you go with me?" Mrinmoyee nodded her head, ran to her room, bolted it from inside, fell down on her bed and holding a pillow close to her heart, laughed embarrassedly. Then, she cried.

Without informing Apoorva, the two ladies started for Kolkata. Reaching there, they stayed at Apoorva's brother-in-law's house.

Disappointed at not receiving Mrinmoyee's letter, Apoorva decided to break his pledge and sat down to write to her. He was looking for such an address that would show his love and also express his disappointment. Just then, he received a letter from his brother-in-law. It said, "Mother's here. Come soon and stay for dinner. Rest is all okay." He immediately went to his sister's house.

The moment he met his mother, he asked, "I hope everything is fine mother!" Mother said, "Yes. You did not come home for the vacation, that's why I have come to take you."

Apoorva said, "Was it necessary to take so much trouble for that? I'm studying for the law exam."

At dinner, Apoorva's sister asked, "*Dada*, why did you not bring *Bowdi* (sister-in-law) with you?"

In a serious tone, the brother said, "Studying for law..."

His brother-in-law laughed and said, "That's all a lie. He did not have the courage to bring her."

His family just kept joking, but Apoorva remained quiet. He did not like anything. All he kept thinking was, "Mrinmoyee could easily have come with mother if she wanted to. Mother may even have tried, but probably, she did not agree." He was too embarrassed to ask mother anything about this.

When dinner ended, there was a storm followed by heavy showers.

Apoorva's sister said, "*Dada*, stay with us tonight."

The brother said, "No. I have to go back home. There's a lot of work."

The brother-in-law said, "What work do you have, so late in the night? If you spend one night here, you will not have to answer anyone. Why worry?" After a lot of coaxing, Apoorva finally agreed to spend the night there.

His sister said, "*Dada*, you look tired. Don't delay. Go to sleep." That is what Apoorva wanted too. All he wanted was to be left alone—he did not want to talk to anyone.

As he came to the entrance of the room, he saw that it was dark. His sister said, "I think the storm has blown the light off. Shall I get you a light, *Dada*?"

Apoorva said, "No, it is not required. I don't keep a light at night." The sister went away. Just as Apoorva was about to enter his bed, he felt two hands embracing him. Before he could express his surprise, he felt a kiss. At first, Apoorva was surprised. Then he understood that his efforts had finally borne fruit.

10

THE LAST TROPHY

IT was the Prize Distribution Day for the I.A. (Class XI) and Matric (Class X) classes. There was a student named Bimala. She was famous for her beauty. She was in-charge of the prizes. She was surrounded by people and was feeling very important, very conceited.

One shy, innocent boy was standing in a corner. As soon as he gained enough courage to come close, it was noticed that he had a wound on his leg. This wound had been bandaged with a dirty cloth. When she saw him, Bimala made a face and said, "Why is he here? He ought to go to the hospital." The boy was heart-broken. Slowly, he went away from there.

He came home, sat in a corner and started weeping. His sister walked in with his breakfast. Seeing him sitting thus, she said, "What is this Jagdish, why are you crying?" When she heard how he had been insulted, she started burning with rage. She said, "Bimala is very conceited about her beauty. My name shall cease to be Mrinalini if, one day, she does not come and touch these very feet of yours."

Many years had passed by since then. The sister was now the Inspector of schools. She told the girls of the school, the story of her brother. The girls abhorred such an act and said that no girl could be so heartless—-even if she was the most beautiful girl.

Mrinalini said, "That which ought not to be the truth,

sometimes turns out to be the truth."

Today is Prize Distribution Day once again. Just a little before the programme, Mrinalini asked the girls, "Alright. That day, the boy who was sent away after being insulted—what position of his would make you happy today?"

Some said "Poet," some said "Revolutionary." An outside girl, who had been invited said, "High Court Judge."

The bell rang and everyone sat down properly. The Chief Guest, who was to give away the prizes, arrived. He was Jagdish Prasad, a High Court Judge. As soon as he sat down, the girl who had been invited, who used to teach Math to Class III students of Muzaffarpur Girls High School, came and placed a garland of flowers at his feet. Taken aback, Jagdish Prasad said, "What kind of respect is this?"

Mrinalini said, "Why do you say it is new? It is very old. In our country, we show our respect to god by beginning to worship Him from his feet. Today, your post has been given the same respect."

Now, let me complete the introduction. This girl was the conceited beauty queen of her time. After her father's death, she has taken on the responsibility of teaching the class. She also does a few tuitions to earn a living. She has been specially invited today to pay respect at the feet that she had abhorred one day.

It seems like a story but sometimes, stories are true. The person, who is writing this history, is Avinash—the boy who had won the biggest prize for reciting Rabindranath Tagore's *Pancha nadeer teere*.

11

RASHMONI'S SON

I

RASHMONI was Kalipada's mother but circumstances had compelled her to take over the onus of the head of the family. Rashmoni's husband, Bhawani Charan, loved his son very much and could not discipline his child at all.

Bhawani Charan had been born into a well-known rich family of Shaniari. Shyama Charan, father of Bhawani Charan, was the son of the first wife of Abhaya Charan. When Abhaya Charan became a widower, he decided to remarry. It was then that his father-in-law had got some property renamed in favour of his daughter. Calculating his son-in-law's age, he had thought that if his daughter was to be widowed, then she would not have to be dependent on her stepson. Shortly after Bhawani Charan's birth, his son-in-law died. Then, he too died.

At that time, Shyama Charan was quite old. In fact, his eldest son was himself one year older than Bhawani. Shyama Charan started bringing up Bhawani along with his sons. He never took even a paisa from Bhawani's mother's property. In fact, he used to show all the accounts to his mother. Everyone admired his honesty. It was for this reason only that his mother, Brajasundari, used to trust Shyama Charan like her own son. In fact, she often used to abuse him for treating her property as separate.

"Son, all this is yours only. I shall not take this property with me to heaven. I don't need to see the accounts." But, Shyama Charan did not pay any heed. He used to keep his sons under strict discipline but he had no control over Bhawani Charan—hence everyone used to say that Shyama Charan loved Bhawani Charan more than his own sons. Therefore, Bhawani did not study and became completely dependent on his brother. He never had to worry about the ancestral property—except sign a few times.

On the other hand, Shyama Charan's eldest son Tarapada used to be by his father's side all the time. As such, he became efficient in his work. After Shyama Charan's death, Tarapada said to Bhawani Charan, "Uncle, we shall not be able to live together any more. You never know, we might have a difference of opinion some day, and then the family may break up."

Bhawani could not ever have dreamt that some day, the family may break up and he'd have to take care of himself. He had always thought that the family, in which he had been brought up, was indivisible. Hence, news that it might break up was really unnerving. When none could convince Tarapada against a break up, Bhawani had to prepare himself for a partition.

Seeing his uncle's worry, Tarapada said, "What's up, uncle? Why do you worry so much? The property is already divided since the time of grandfather."

Bhawani was amazed. He said, "Is that so? I didn't know anything about it. What about this house?"

Tarapada said, "If you want to, you can keep the house. Just give us the house in the front and we won't want anything."

When Bhawani told his mother about it, she hit her forehead and said, "What's that? I had got that portion as the bride's property. Besides, it does not even fetch us that much income. And why won't you get your share in the ancestral property? My husband had himself got his will written in duplicate—one was given to me. It is in my trunk." The trunk was opened. The papers of the gifting of *Alandi Taluq* were there, but there was no will. The will had been stolen. An advisor was called. His name was Bagala Charan. Everyone said that he was very clever.

He said, "So what, if the will is not found? The two brothers will have an equal share in the father's property."

Just then, the will was produced from the other side. It did not give any portion to Bhawani Charan. According to the will, the entire property had been given to the grandson, Tarapada's son, before the birth of Bhawani. Bhawani filed a case. After many pleadings, the court alloted only the middle portion of the house to Bhawani. However, Bhawani was happy with the judgement. Tarapada shifted to the front portion of the house. And, the families stopped seeing each other.

II

Shyama Charan's deceit upset Brajasundari a great deal. He had been unjust and had stolen her husband's will, thereby hurting his father's trust. He had not given the share to his brother. She could just not get herself to forget it. Every day of her life, she used to heave sighs and say, "God will never forgive him." She would often assure Bhawani by saying, "I don't understand the law or the courts. I'm telling you, my husband's will shall not remain covered for long. You shall definitely get it back." This would give Bhawani a lot of consolation. This assurance became even more assuring after his mother's death. It was his belief that his condition would improve some day.

Instead of the fine quality *Dhakai dhoti*, he started wearing coarse material and did not celebrate *Puja.* To himself, he said, "These people don't realise that all this gaiety is for a few days only—and then, there will be nothing." He would discuss all this with the servants. The only thing that worried Bhawani was that who would inherit his property when he died? He hadn't had a son until now.

Now, when the son was born, everyone said, "Now fortune will once again smile on this household. Late Abhaya Charan has once again taken birth into this house." The boy had the same eyes. The boy's horoscope also said that he'd be able to get back the lost property. Some changes were noted in Bhawani Charan after the birth of the son. Until now, he had not cared much for his poverty but now, he was not able to maintain that attitude—after all, his son was involved now. He felt that he had cheated his son.

His wife, Rashmoni, was a different kind of a person. She did not care much for the Chaudhary family of Shaniari. Bhawani was aware of it and would laugh about it. He knew that with the kind of family his wife had grown in, it was difficult for her to imagine the fame of the Choudharys. She'd say, "I come from a poor family. May God give my Kalipada a long life! He is my biggest wealth!" She never believed that the will would be found again and that Kalipada would be a rich man. There was not a man in the village with whom her husband would not discuss the lost will. The only person he would not discuss it with, was his wife for she would did not find any interest in it. The future and the past glory was way beyond—the only thing she'd worry about was the present.

She had to run the household with great difficulty. Her husband, Bhawani Charan, was not the kind of person who would send people away because of shortage of money. However, the people who would take refuge in Bhawani Charan's house would never help her in her work. They would feel insulted if they were asked to work. Besides, Bhawani Charan used to believe that if one took work from a person who had taken refuge under him, then, it was like giving him a job—it lost the beauty of giving charity or refuge.

Hence, it was on Rashmoni to fulfil the shortages of this family. Living in scarcity and fighting poverty, makes one hard—one loses one's charm. Those, for whom she slogged, could not tolerate her. Not that she just cooked for the family, she even took the burden of getting the grain. Bhawani Charan would never ask anyone to return his money, while Rashmoni would never give anyone a concession of even one paisa. For this, the people hated her. In fact, even her husband, in a soft voice, sometimes criticised her and said that her miserliness and her crude behaviour brought a bad name to his famous family. She, however, ignored it all and continued doing whatever work she was doing. No one dared hinder her work.

She never asked her husband to do any work. On the contrary, she was always afraid; he might interfere in her work. For a long time, Rashmoni did not have a child. So, she cared for her husband like a son. Hence, after her mother-in-law's death, she had to take on the onus of the head of the family as well as the lady of the house. She had to protect her husband from all difficulties including her elder brother-in-law's son. Until now, Bhawani Charan had acted as per her directions only. However, now it became difficult to follow her, so far as Kalipada was concerned. The reason was that Rashmoni did not look upon her son as Bhawani Charan did. So far as her husband was concerned, she'd think, "It's not his fault! He was born in a well-to-do family. There is no other alternative." Hence, she never expected her husband to suffer any problem.

Her accounts, as for people at home and outsiders, were very stern; but for Bhawani Charan she was very liberal. If, for some reason, there'd be any problem because of scarcity, she'd never let her husband know that. She'd probably say, "The stupid dog spoilt everything by licking the food," and she'd curse her carelessness. Or else, she'd put the blame on Natabihari and Bhawani Charan would try to save him from his wife's anger.

Rashmoni could forgive her husband for anything, but not for his behaviour with the son. After all, he had taken birth from her womb only—how could he behave like a lord? He should be a hard-working man—he'd have to work hard and suffer too. However, she took care of his food and clothing. She had also arranged a teacher for him and had told the teacher not to show any kind of laxity.

Of late, Bhawani Charan had started showing signs of rebellion, but Rashmoni could not see through it. Bhawani could not tolerate that the son of this house would not ever eat dry pounded rice, while the son of the other house would eat rice pudding.

For the pujas, Rashmoni had bought clothes made out of the coarse cloth that even servants objected to. She tried her best to make her husband understand her. She would say, "Kalipada is happy with whatever he has got. Then why do you always have a grudge?" However, Bhawani Charan was never able to reconcile that just because Kalipada did not know about his family glory, he had to suffer. Actually the way he would come about dancing to show even a little gift that he would get would upset Bhawani Charan. He could never bear it. So, he had to turn his face and walk away.

Once, Bagala Charan brought an amazing statue of a lady. When its key was applied, the lady would leave her chain and fan herself at a great speed. Kalipada was greatly attracted to it. He knew his mother very well. That's why, without saying a word to his mother, he went to Bhawani Charan and made his request. Bhawani Charan immediately promised it to him but was shocked to hear the price. Yet, he went and stood before his wife like a beggar. He spoke of various things and then finally, made his request. Very curtly, Rashmoni said, "You've gone mad!"

Bhawani Charan became quiet and contemplated for a while. Then, he said, "Alright, see. There's no need to give me *ghee* and *payas* with my meals. They say that it causes acidity. I have told you to stop giving me pooris at night. I'd much rather have rice."

Rashmoni said, "I have not seen you being harmed because of food. You have grown up eating pooris."

Bhawani Charan was willing to make all types of sacrifices, but his wife was very strict. Bhawani Charan could see no way to buy the statue for his son. One day, he went to his brother's house and after a lot of polite conversation, asked about that statue. He knew that there was no reason to keep his financial condition a secret from Bagala Charan. He took out an old and expensive *jamawar* which he was hiding under the shawl and said, "Going through bad times. That is why I do not have much cash. I have come to mortgage this *jamawar* to take the doll for Kalipada."

It would not have hurt Bagala Charan if there was anything less expensive than the *jamawar*, but he knew that he would not be able to digest it. Not only would the villagers criticise him, even Rashmoni would not spare him. So, he refused the deal.

Every day Kalipada would ask him about the doll and he'd say, "Wait till the seventh day." Under some pretext, he went indoors. Then, suddenly, he said, "I have been noticing for some time that Kalipada has started looking sickish." Rashmoni said, "No. I have not seen any signs of sickness. He's probably thinking about some mischief somewhere." Bhawani Charan came out patting his head. He sat and chewed tobacco.

On the fifth day of the *puja* also, he did not eat anything. He said he was not hungry. On the sixth day, Rashmoni herself called Kalipada, addressing him by his nickname. She said, "Bhentu, you've grown in years, yet you have not stopped making your demands. Do you know that if you desire to have something which you cannot have, it's half stealing?"

Kalipada replied, "How do I know? Baba had promised he'd give it to me." Rashmoni sat down to explain what his father meant when he said so. She had never explained anything like that before. Whatever she said was short and stern. She never needed to say anything softly. That is why Kalipada was surprised at her behaviour today. But, what could he do? It was very difficult to shift his mind from that doll. He picked up a stick and started poking it on the ground. At this, Rashmoni returned to her stern mood and said, "I don't care if you lose your temper or cry! You will not get what you are not supposed to get." And, without wasting any more time, she quickly went inside to attend to the other household chores. Kalipada too, went out.

Bhawani Charan, at that time, was sitting alone and chewing tobacco. When he saw Kalipada, he immediately started walking towards him. Kalipada asked him for his doll. Bhawani Charan did not say anything. Only, he embraced him and said, "Wait son. I have some work. Let me finish that, and then we'll talk." And he went out. Kalipada understood that his father did not have any work anywhere. He came inside and said, "Mother, I do not want that doll that fans itself."

Mother was cutting betel nut at that time. She was thrilled. God knows what transpired between the mother and the son, but Rashmoni immediately left for Bagala Charan's house. Bhawani

Charan came back very late that night. Rashmoni brought before him a box of papers that had been tied with a string. She went and kept them in his room. It was only after having his meal that he noticed it. That's how she had planned it. After the meal he had said, "The food was excellent today. I had not eaten such tasty fish curry in a very long time. So was the curd."

On the seventh day, Kalipada got the result of his long standing desire. The whole day, he saw the doll fanning itself. Under normal circumstances, he would have got tired watching the same doll so many times but Rashmoni had got it on rent for one day only, by paying Rs. 2. So, on the eighth day, Kalipada sighed, put the doll into the box and himself, went and returned the doll to Bagala Charan.

From then onwards, he became a follower of his mother. From then onwards, Bhawani Charan would give Kalipada some expensive gifts on *puja* that would amaze him. Slowly, Kalipada matured and realised that nothing can be achieved in this world without giving something. He realised that his duty was not to increase the burden but to take on the burden of the family.

Realising this, he started studying hard for a scholarship. When he succeeded in getting a scholarship, Bhawani Charan felt that he didn't need to study further—that he should take care of their business. Kalipada told his mother that he would not be able to learn anything if he did not go to Kolkata to study. His mother agreed with him. He assured her that they would not have to spend any money—that the scholarship would suffice and that he'd take on some job there too. It was difficult to get Bhawani Charan to agree. He could not get himself to say that there wasn't any property that needed looking after. He also said that the Chaudharys had managed until now, without going out. Finally, Bagala Charan, the wisest man in the village, also agreed with Rashmoni. He said that Kalipada would, one day, come back as an advocate and get back the property. This consoled Bhawani Charan to a great extent. He started talking to Kalipada about the will. He would listen to his mother's advice but did not care much for his father's advice.

The day before he was to leave for Kolkata, Rashmoni put a *raksha kavach* around his neck and, putting a fifty-rupee note in his hand, said, "Keep this note—use it when you are in dire need." Kalipada accepted it with great reverence because it had been saved with great difficulty, from everyday expenses. He promised himself that he would never spend the note but keep it as his mother's blessings.

III

One could not hear Bhawani Charan talk about the theft of the will so often now. All he talked about now was Kalipada. He went around the locality talking about him. With specs on his nose, he'd go to various houses, reading the letter. He'd say, "Can you hear me? I have just received a letter from Kalipada. A second bridge is being built over the Ganges near the Hoogly."

Kalipada shared a room with someone. To meet his expenses he would teach children; at night, he'd do the ledger work. After the lapsing of the initial scholarship, he cleared the entrance exam and had once again, was given a scholarship. Thrilled at his son's success and at the fact that he was now on the verge of getting a job, Bhawani Charan wanted to invite the whole village for a meal. However, not getting any encouragement from Rashmoni, he shelved the idea.

Kalipada had now shifted to a mess near the college. The mess in-charge gave him a room on the ground floor. It was a convenient room although it was damp. All he had to do was to teach the son of the mess in-charge and he'd be given meals twice a day. He had no contact with anyone living there, although he did realise that he needed their friendship.

Shailendra was the head on the upper storeys; hence, contact with him was necessary. He was the son of a big shot. It was not necessary for him to live in the hostel, yet he loved it because he loved to live with a number of students. With the residents of the hostel, he could enjoy himself without any responsibility. Shailendra was a very soft-hearted man. He liked to help people get rid of their sorrows, but at the same time if someone did not take his refuge, he'd not leave him without giving him immense sorrow. When his kindness became cruel, it would be ghastly.

Poor Kalipada continued to stay in his damp room only. Wearing a torn vest, he'd sit on his mat and try to memorise his lesson because whatever might happen, he must get his scholarship regularly.

Before coming to Kolkata, his mother had made him promise that he would not mix with the sons of big shots. He had never been close to Shailendra and even if he knew that most of his problems would be solved if he were close to Shailendra, he did not feel the attraction to go close to Shailendra, who could not bear his conceit. Besides, Kalipada's poverty showed in his lifestyle, his clothes. He even used to pray both morning and evening. In order to find out more about this 'villager', two or three boys from Shailendra's side had been loitering around in front of his room, but they were not able to compel him to speak. They invited him to dinner but he refused, saying that he was not used to it.

For a few days, he was greatly disturbed by the loud sound of music and by the banging on the floors. He could not concentrate on his studies. So, during the day, he used to carry his books to the river bank, sit under a tree and study and at night, he used to stay awake till late for study.

Due to the problem of food and residence, Kalipada soon developed a migraine which was so bad that it would sometimes keep him confined to bed for three-four days. He knew that if his father would come to know about it, he would definitely not let him stay there, or would himself, come down to live here. Bhawani Charan, on the other and, was under the impression that his son was so happy and comfortable that the villagers could not even dream of. He was under the impression that comforts in Kolkata grew on their own, just as the trees in the villages did, and that everyone could enjoy the fruits of it—Kalipada did not want to disillusion him either. Even during his illness, he never wrote about it to his father.

It used to just become intolerable for him when even during

his illness, Shailendra's gang used to trouble him. He'd spend nights tossing and turning in bed, calling out to his mother. The more he suffered on account of his poverty, the more determined he would become to free his parents from this curse. He decided that if he got a good scholarship in his F.A. (Fellow of Arts, equivalent to grade XI-XII), he'd leave this hostel and go elsewhere; but, although he did not fail, he didn't get the scholarship.

People on the top had thought that Kalipada would leave the hostel after the vacations, but he did not.

Earlier, he used to keep his room open. The boys from the upper floor used to come, open his room and criticise his parents for the not-so-civilised way in which his parents used to give him snacks, etc. Kalipada could bear anything but his parents being criticised or insulted. So this time, even if he went out of his room for five minutes, he'd lock it. Shailendra and the others could not tolerate it. They criticised Kalipada and said that he seemed to be the next 'Bank of Bengal'.

Shailendra had never entered Kalipada's room. So, he told his gang to find out what wealth Kalipada had brought with him this time. Everyone got excited about it. The lock was not a very strong one. It could be opened with any key.

One evening, when Kalipada had gone to give tuitions, two-three young boys opened the lock and, with a lantern, entered Kalipada's room. They discovered the containers of pickles, etc., but did not feel that these were the priceless things that he was trying to hide.

Then, they found a key. They opened his trunk and ransacked it, but did not find anything except dirty clothes. They were about to go when they saw something wrapped in a handkerchief, under his clothes. They opened it and found a fifty-rupee note in it. They all burst out laughing because they felt that Kalipada had been locking his room up for this note only. Just then, they heard a cough like Kalipada's. They immediately shut the box and holding the fifty-rupee note in their hands, they rushed out. One of them quickly locked the room. Shailendra too laughed at the note. They all wanted to see how Kalipada would react when he found the note missing. After teaching the students, when Kalipada returned at night, he did not notice anything. Besides, he was having a massive headache.

The next day, he pulled out his trunk and was shocked to see that it was open. Although he was, by nature, not careless, he thought that maybe he had forgotten to lock his trunk, because if a thief had come, he would have broken the lock too. Then, as he opened the trunk, he saw that his clothes had been turned topsy-turvy and his fifty-rupee note was missing. He looked everywhere, but did not find it.

When he finally lost all hope of getting the note and the headache also would not leave him, he lay down on his bed like a dead man. His mother must have gone through a lot of trouble to collect this note. He could hear footsteps coming down and climbing up the steps, as the boys of Shailendra's gang came, saw and again went up to tell what was happening. On hearing the laughter from above, Kalipada realised it was not a thief's doing. It did not take him a moment to realise that Shailendra's gang had taken the note out of curiosity. It would not have hurt him so much if a thief had taken it away. He felt as if some vain youth had raised his hand on his mother. All these days, Kalipada had never climbed the steps and gone up; today anger got the better of him and with a face red with rage, he ran up the steps.

Today was Sunday. There was no reason for him to go to college. The boys were all sitting—some on stools, some on chairs and the rest on the floor—and gossiping. Standing in the middle, Kalipada shouted, "Give my note back."

Had he pleaded, he would surely have got the fruit of it, but seeing his angry face, Shailendra got irritated. Had his guard been there, he would have asked him to throw this uncivilised boy out of this place, but this was not his house. All of them got up and shouted together, "What are you talking about? What note? Are you trying to say that we are thieves?" If Kalipada had something in his hand, he would have killed someone. Four or five youth came, held his hands and pinned him down. He did not have any proof or the strength to oppose this injustice—everyone said that his suspicion was baseless.

How he spent that night, only Kalipada knows. Shailendra took out a hundred-rupee note and said, "Go and give this to the *Bangaal*!" His friends said, "He's gone mad! Let him first get rid of his anger. He'll have to give a written apology to each of us first, then, we'll consider it." And they all went off to sleep.

By morning, everyone had practically forgotten about Kalipada. A few people, while coming down the steps, could hear voices from his room. They thought that he was probably taking advice from a lawyer. As it was locked from inside, they put their ears to the door and tried to listen, but they heard no legal talk, only lamenting. They went upward and informed Shailendra accordingly.

Shailendra came down and stood outside the door. He could not make out what Kalipada was saying except that at regular intervals, he was shouting out for his father. He felt scared—what if he had gone mad because of the grief for the note? He shouted out his name from outside, two or three times. "Kalipada Babu!" but did not get any reply. He shouted once again, "Kalipada Babu! Open the door. That note of yours has been found." But, the door did not open. Shailendra had not imagined that things would become so bad. He did not show his regret before his followers. Finally, he said, "Let us break open the door!" Someone suggested, "Let's call the police. What if he has actually turned mad and tries to harm us? I'm scared!"

Shailendra said, "No. Someone go quickly and call Dr. Anadi." The doctor stayed close by. They broke open the door and went inside. They saw that the bedding was half on the bed and half on the ground. Kalipada was lying unconscious on the floor. His eyes were open. They were bloodshot—as red as his face. The doctor sat down beside him and examined him for a long time. Then, he asked Shailendra, "Does he has any relatives?" Shailendra was scared. He asked, "Why? What's the matter?"

The doctor said, "It's good to inform them. The symptoms are not good."

Shailendra said, "We don't know him very well, but, we'll find out. But, what can we do till then?"

The doctor said, "He needs to be immediately shifted to a good room on the first floor. Besides, a 24-hour nurse should also be arranged for."

Shailendra took the patient to his room. He told his friends not to crowd around Kalipada and so, asked them to leave the room. Then he put an ice bag on his head and started fanning him.

In order to find out his address, his trunk had to be opened once again. Shailendra found two piles of letters in it—one from his mother and the other from his father. He brought them to his room, sat on the patient's bed and started reading them. He was taken aback to see the address. Then he saw the writer's name—Bhawani Charan Devsharma. He put the letter away and continued staring at Kalipada's face. A few days back one of his friends had said that he had some resemblance to Kalipada, but he had not liked it. Now, he realised that it was not nonsense—his grandfather had two brothers—Shyama Charan and Bhawani Charan. He did not know anything else because it was never discussed at home. He did not even know that Bhawani Charan had a son called Kalipada! And that this Kalipada was his paternal uncle!

Now, it all came back to Shailendra. He remembered that his grandmother always spoke very highly and lovingly of Bhawani Charan, who was actually her brother-in-law but young enough to be her son. She knew that Bhawani Charan was a simple man. She used to say, "You people have cheated him. I do not believe that my father-in-law did not give him a share in his property because he loved him a lot." Shailendra remembered that he too, like his uncle, used to get irritated by what his grandmother said. Shailendra did not know what a poor condition Bhawani Charan was in now. Seeing Kalipada's condition, he understood everything. And he was glad that Kalipada had not been able to join his gang.

IV

All these days, Shailendra's gang had hurt and insulted Kalipada. Shailendra could not keep his uncle under the same roof. After consulting the doctor, he shifted him to a more comfortable house.

After receiving Shailendra's letter, Bhawani Charan got someone to accompany him and hurriedly came to Kolkata. When he left for Kolkata, Rashmoni had told him, "If you think it is needed, let me know. I'll come immediately." She stayed back and prayed to the family deity.

Bhawani Charan was shocked to see Kalipada's condition. He had still not fully regained consciousness—he called him *master moshai*. Kalipada would often shout out 'Baba'. At this, his father would hold his hand, go close to his face and lovingly say, "Here I am, my son," but he did not seem to recognise him.

The doctor came and said that the fever had gone down a little and that he would now, make progress. Bhawani Charan did not once believe that he may not recover. So, when the doctor said he would recover, he thought that he was recovering and wrote the same to his wife.

Bhawani Charan was amazed at Shailendra's behaviour. Who would say that he was not a close kin? Shailendra gave him a lot of respect. Such behaviour was not expected of a boy from Kolkata.

Soon Kalipada became aware of his surroundings. He was taken aback to see his father at his bedside. He was worried that his father would become the laughing stock for the boys of Kolkata. He looked in all directions but did not seem to recognise this room. But, he didn't have the strength to find out. Maybe his father had taken a better apartment in Kolkata and shifted him there. But, where did he get the money from?

At one point, when his father was not in the room, Shailendra came to him with some fruits. Kalipada stared at him, dumbfounded—wondering if it was some kind of a joke. Shailendra kept the basket of fruits on the table, bent down, touched Kalipada's feet and said, "I have committed a serious offence. Please forgive me."

Kalipada did not know what to do. But he understood that this was a genuine act. He did not say a word—only picked up a fruit and started eating it. Kalipada remembered how he had longed for Shailendra's friendship when he had first come to this hostel.

Kalipada was surprised to see the good relationship between his villager father and Shailendra. Shailendra called him *Thakurdada* and joked with him about the grandmother. Shailendra shamelessly also acknowledged that while Kalipada lay unconscious, he had eaten all the pickles, *aam papad*, etc. that had been prepared by grandmother. Kalipada felt a peculiar satisfaction at hearing this. He kept longing for his mother—she'd be thrilled to see this handsome boy!

Kalipada was ashamed to say that although they were poor today, they once had a lot of property. The fact that they were poor today could not be covered up! Even Bhawani Charan could not take pride in that fact but those were the days when he lived in luxury, the days of his youth. In fact, it carried on till his elder brother's wife was alive. But, off and on, the episode of the will being stolen kept coming to his mind and he would get very agitated. Of course, he had no doubt that the will would be found—his mother's blessings would not go waste. Kalipada knew that this was only his father's whim. It could not come true and he did not want it to be revealed before Shailendra. He had often spoken about it to his father. He had noticed that Shailendra did not like this topic to be talked about.

Bhawani Charan took pride in the fact that his mother was literate. He said that she had kept the paper under lock and key, so how could the will vanish? Kalipada would try to pacify him by saying, "So what, father! If your nephews have taken it, let them enjoy it. After all, they are also the grandsons of your father! It stays in the family only." When Shailendra could not tolerate this talk for very long—he'd walk out. This would upset Kalipada for he felt that Shailendra might consider his father to be a greedy person.

Shailendra would have revealed his identity before Kalipada and Bhawani Charan, but talk of the will being stolen stopped him. He did not want to believe that his father and grandfather had stolen the will but he could not refute the fact that injustice had been meted out to Bhawani Charan. He did not start any argument on this topic—he'd remain absolutely quiet and if he got an opportunity, he'd walk out.

Even now, Kalipada's head would sometimes ache in the evenings but he paid no heed to it. He longed to study. He had lost his scholarship once. He couldn't afford to lose it this time too. He started studying secretly from Shailendra as the doctor had strictly forbidden him to do so.

One day, Kalipada said to Bhawani Charan, "Baba, please go back home. Mother is alone. I have recovered." Shailendra said, "There's no harm in your going back home. There's nothing to worry about. Besides, we are all here."

Bhawani Charan said, "That I know; I know that I needn't worry about Kalipada. There was no need for me to come yet, I couldn't help it. Besides, one cannot but do what your grandmother says."

Shailendra laughed and said, "It's your fault, *Thakurdada*. You have spoilt her."

Bhawani Charan laughed and said, "Alright. I'll see the discipline in your house when your wife comes!"

Kalipada had been well-looked after by Shailendra. No amount of comfort and luxury could replace the care that Shailendra had given to Kalipada. That's why it did not need much convincing for Bhawani Charan to return home.

In the morning, when Shailendra went to Kalipada's room, he saw that his face and eyes were red, his body was as hot as fire. He had not been able to sleep a wink in the night. Kalipada had not yet been able to recover from the weakness. This relapse now got the doctor really worried. He called Shailendra aside and said that his condition was not very good. So, Shailendra went to Bhawani Charan and said, "*Thakurda*, you are worried and so is Kalipada. The patient is probably not getting the right care. Hence, I suggest that you call grandmother here too without further delay." Although he tried not to, yet somehow, his words put a fear in Bhawani Charan's mind. Bhawani Charan's hands started trembling. He said, "Do whatever you think is right."

Rashmoni received the letter. She immediately came to Kolkata with Bagala Charan. She reached in the evening and was able to see Kalipada alive only for a few hours. In an unconscious state, he had called out to his mother a number of times but she could not express her grief for fear of how her husband would survive this calamity.

V

It was midnight. Tired out, Rashmoni had fallen off to sleep for a few minutes but Bhawani Charan could not sleep. Much before he went to Kolkata, Kalipada used to sit in a corner of the room and study. Bhawani Charan took a lamp into that corner. Then he came and sat on the *diwan*. It was a dark night. It had been drizzling. He opened the door and looked out into the garden that Kalipada had worked on. The tree that he had himself planted was still laden with blossoms.

Now there was no hope, nothing to look forward to! No one would come back from college during the vacations. Depressed, he shouted out, "Oh God!" and sat down on the floor. Kalipada had gone to Kolkata saying that he would pull his father out of his poverty—but he had left his father all alone in this world!

Just then, Bhawani Charan heard sounds of footsteps. His heart missed a beat. He felt as if Kalipada had returned to see his garden. But it was raining cats and dogs. He'd get wet. Then he saw someone come and stand before him. His face was covered. It was difficult to recognise him. Bhawani Charan said, "So you've come!" and quickly, went out to open the door, but there was no one there. He shouted out Kalipada's name loudly. The servant came out and, with great difficulty, took him in.

In the morning, when the servant went to sweep the house, he saw a bundle lying there. He brought it and gave it to Bhawani

Charan. He opened it and saw something like an old testimonial. He wore his specs, read a little, immediately rushed to Rashmoni and held the paper in front of her.

Rashmoni asked, "What is it?"

Bhawani Charan said, "That will."

Rashmoni said, "Who gave it?"

Bhawani Charan said, "He had come last night. He gave it."

Rashmoni asked, "What'll we do with it?"

Bhawani Charan said, "Now I don't need it." He tore the will to pieces and threw it away. When it became known, Bagala Charan said, "Did I not say that Kalipada would be able to retrieve the will?"

The grocer Ram Charan said, "But when the train arrived at 10 p.m., I saw a handsome youth with this paper. He was asking me the way to the house of the Chaudharys."

12

TARAPRASANNA'S FAME

FOR a writer, Taraprasanna was a little shy and lazy. He hated going out before people. As he used to sit at home and write, his vision was not very clear, he bent a little and had even less experience of worldly matters. People also found him a little strange but they too, could not be blamed. Obviously, if a person said he was really glad to meet him, Taraprasanna would continue admiring his right palm as if to say "So what? You may have had the pleasure but I cannot say the same for myself." When someone praised his voice, he remained silent as if to say that he acknowledged it.

His wife, Dakshayani too, could not reach upto his standards. She would often say, "Alright, Alright! I accept defeat. I have other works to attend to—how many men have the good fortune of having a wife who accepts defeat?"

Taraprasanna's-days were passing very well. It was Dakshayani's strong belief that there was no one to compare with her husband in intelligence and ability and she never hesitated in saying so. Hearing this, Taraprasanna would also say, "There is no one like your husband. Who will you compare him with?"

This would really anger Dakshayani. She however, had only one regret—that her husband's capabilities had not come to the forefront—that he had not made any effort to do so. He never got his writings published! She would often request her husband to read out his writings to her—she would, very often, not understand them, but they would amaze her all the same. She had read the *Ramayana* and the *Mahabharata*, and understood them; but she had never read writings like her husband's.

She would imagine that when the book was published and no one would understand a word, then it would create such amazement! Thousands of times she had asked him to get his writings published.

Taraprasanna had four children—all daughters. Dakshayani would think that it was her fault. Hence, she used to consider herself as the most incapable wife for such a brilliant husband.

When the first daughter became older, Taraprasanna could no longer stay carefree. He realised that he would have to marry off one daughter after another—and that would require money! His wife said, "If you pursue your work seriously, you'll not have to worry! Let's go to Kolkata and get your writings published. Let a few people know you. Then let's see whether money comes in or not!"

Slowly, Taraprasanna started believing his wife's belief and felt that once he was able to publish all his writings, he would get so much of money that he'd even be able to get all the daughters of the neighbourhood married off!

When he was about to leave for Kolkata, Dakshayani realised that she could not let him go alone. Who would look after him? But, her husband was not willing to take his wife and daughters to a new place. Finally, Dakshayani appointed a clever man from the neighbourhood to take her place and go with her husband to Kolkata. Then, after giving both of them a number of instructions, she bade them goodbye.

Taraprasanna came to Kolkata and with the assistance of this clever man, brought out a book called *Vedanta Prabhakar*. He had already spent the majority of the money he had got by mortgaging his wife's jewellery. He sent a copy of this to all the small and big editors for the review. He sent the copies of the book to all the leading booksellers. And, he also sent one copy to his wife.

The day his wife read her husband's name printed on top

of the book, she invited all the women of the neighbourhood to a meal and kept the book where everyone was to sit. And when everyone came and sat there, she yelled out loudly, "Oh my God! Who has kept the book there? Annada, please pass the book, I'll put it away." Then, she took the book and kept it away. After a moment, she went to pick up something else and dropped the book. Then, addressing her daughter, she said, "Shashi! You want to read father's book, is it? Then, why are you feeling embarrassed? Take it and read it!" Then, after another moment, she said, "Don't keep your father's book like that! Give it to Kamala *didi.* She'll put it on top of the *almirah.*"

Then, book reviews started appearing in the papers. They were very much as expected. Although they may not have understood even a word of it, the critics said, "Never before had such a book been published." Those who could not even touch another book besides the *Bangla* translation of Reynolds's *London Mystery* wrote very excitedly, "If, instead of innumerable dramas and novels, one or two such epics are published now and then, then *Bangla* literature would definitely be worth reading."

Only one who had never heard the name of *Vedanta*, said, "We do not agree with all that Taraprasanna *Babu* has said—we do not mention it due to lack of space." His *Vedanta Prabhakar* could be found in all libraries of the country. Just at the time when Taraprasanna was thrilled with his success, he received a letter telling him that his wife Dakshayani would soon be giving birth to her fifth child. So, he went to one bookseller to get money. All the booksellers said in one voice that not even one copy had been sold. Only at one place he heard that someone from some remote area had asked for one copy of the book and that it had been sent by VPP but, the book had come back—he had to pay the demurrage. So, in anger, he offered to return. The author was perplexed. He was unable to understand why this happened. Then, with the little money he had left, he went home.

He went to his wife and expressed his joy. Dakshayani had been waiting for the good news. Then he gave her copies of *Navaprabhat, Yugantar, Bharatabhagyachakra, Shubhajagaran* and many other and said that there were many more papers. His wife, however, said that she would see the others in the evening. Then, Taraprasanna said, "This time in Kolkata, I heard that the Lord Saheb's wife had brought out a paper, but it did not say anything about *Vedanta Prabhakar*."

His wife said, "I didn't ask about that. What else have you brought? I mean, how much money have you brought?"

Taraprasanna said, "I have borrowed Rs. 5 from Vidhubhushan." Finally, when Dakshayani heard everything, then all her faith on the goodness of this world was shattered. She was sure that the booksellers had cheated her husband.

Suddenly, she felt that Vidhubhushan, whom she had so trustingly sent with her husband, had been in touch with the booksellers and Chatterjee, was her husband's greatest enemy. All this was definitely his doing.

Dakshayani's worries regarding her family continued to increase. When this method of earning money failed, she had to take even greater blame for the birth of the daughters.

At the time of delivery, Dakshayani's condition became very bad. Helpless, Taraprasanna went to Vidhubhushan and said, "Please keep as mortgage these few books of mine and give me some money so that I can call a midwife from the city."

Vidhubhushan said, "Don't worry about it. I shall give you all the money you need. Take away the books." After collecting money, Vidhubhushan himself went and brought the midwife.

Before delivery, Dakshayani called her husband into the room and made him promise, "Whenever you feel the pain, do not forget to have the medicine. And don't open the *maduli* that the sage gave to you." Then, she said that she did not have any faith in Vidhubhushan, that he was the one who had ruined her husband's life. After this, she told her husband to beware of the cunning. Then, softly, she said, "See, if my daughter survives, name her Vedantaprabha. After that, you may address her as Prabha only."

After saying this, she paid her respects to her husband and, in her mind, said, "I had come to my husband's house only to give birth to daughters. Now, it seems that I have got over with my job."

When the midwife said, "Look at her once. See what a beautiful daughter you have given birth to," the mother opened her eyes, looked at her daughter and lovingly said, "Vedantaprabha." Then, she became speechless.

13

THE HUNGRY STONE

MY relatives and I were returning to Kolkata after the vacation, when we met *Babuji* in the train. Seeing the way he was dressed, I initially mistook him for a Muslim. He started discussing all the things of the world as if the creator had made all his creations after discussing them with him. This was the first time we were going out, and had not met many people on the train. So, we were amazed at the way he was behaving. In fact, my theosophist relative strongly believed that this co-passenger of ours certainly had some mystique or divine power about him—some kind of magnetism! He was listening spellbound, to whatever he said and was even noting down some statements he made. I have a feeling that extraordinary human being also noted it and was very happy about it.

When the train stopped at the junction, we all got off to wait for the second connecting train. So, we proceeded towards the waiting room. It was 10:30 p.m. We heard that the train was coming in quite late due to some mishap on the way. I decided to join the tables and sleep on them, when this gentleman came up with the following story. That night, I could not get any sleep....

Because of some differences of opinion, I had left my job at Junagarh and joined service at the Nizam's in Hyderabad. I was posted in Bareech, which is an extremely beautiful place. The Shusta river flows through the dense forests below the mountains. There is a white palace on the banks of this river—

standing all alone; isolated from habitation. The market place and the village of Bareech are far from this place.

Approximately 250 years ago Shah Mahmud II had constructed this palace far away from the city for his pleasure. At that time, very fresh water used to flow out of the fountains. Women, with long flowing hair, used to walk on the banks before their bath. They would sing *ghazals* and play the sitar.

Now, there is neither fountain nor the songs nor do the beautiful streams fall on the white marble floor. Now, it is the residence of the collector. However, the old employee of the office, Karim Khan had, again and again, forbidden me to live in that house. He had said, "If you desire to, stay during the day but never at night." I had laughed it off. Even the workers refused to work here at night. I agreed. This house was so notorious that even thieves refused to come here at night. At the beginning, it really weighed on me. I'd try to work outside till as late as possible and then, tired out, I used to come back and go off to sleep.

But slowly, before the end of the week, an inexplicable intoxication started attacking me. It is difficult to explain that state of mind and difficult to make people believe it. It seems that the process had started the moment I set foot into this house, but I clearly and vividly remember the day I felt it first.

It was the beginning of summer; I had no work in hand. It was just a little before sunset. I was sitting on the ground floor of the house on the banks of the river. There was no breeze. A strong perfume was coming from the *Tulsi*, and mint jungles and had covered the entire area. Just then, the sun hid behind the mountains and it became dark. I was just contemplating getting up and roaming around when I heard footsteps on the stairs. I turned around, but saw none.

I thought it was just my imagination. So, I once again, came and sat down. Just then, I heard the footsteps of a number of feet—as if lots of them were coming down together. I was terrified. Although I did not see even one figure, yet, I felt as if a group of women had climbed down into the Shusta to have a bath on this hot summer day. But, they did not even notice me.

I don't know whether it was fear or joy or curiosity, but I felt an excitement. I longed to see them but there was none before me. I thought that if I tried, I would be able to hear all their talk very clearly. It seemed as if dancers of the third century were moving before me. Feeling scared, I raised my eyes and looked inside—it seemed as if there was an assembly but it was so dark that I could not see anything. I thought that I must eat to my full because all kinds of diseases attack an empty stomach. So, I called the cook and asked him to prepare a *Mughlai* meal for me. The next morning, I found all this quite amusing.

The next day was the day to write the quarterly report. So, I was supposed to work till late in the night. But, something kept pulling me towards the house. I felt as if everyone was waiting for me. Leaving the report incomplete, I walked through the dark, dense forest and reached the house.

There was a big room right in front of the house. It was always empty; but today, as I pushed the door open and entered, it seemed as if a big rebellion had taken place—as if all the people had run to any direction they found place in. So, I just stood there. I could smell *itr*. I stood in the middle of that huge, dark, lonely hall and heard the sound of fountain water falling on the white marble floor; the sound of the sitar being played, of anklets, of the clock and the sound of the *bulbul* calling out from the cage… an illusionary world was being created before me!

And I stood there, in the middle of it all, feeling as if all this was real and everything else was an illusion. That I was me, so-and-so's eldest son, that I earn Rs 450 per month and travel by carriage—all started seeming strange to me. And I stood there and laughed loudly!

Just then, my Muslim caretaker entered the room with a lamp. I don't know whether he thought me mad or not but I was brought back to reality and soon I gained consciousness. So, I read the newspaper, had my food and after putting out the lights lay down. I didn't know when I went off to sleep or for how long I had slept. Suddenly I woke up with a shiver. There was no sound, nor had I seen anyone enter the room, yet, somehow, I felt as if someone was pushing me slowly. When I woke up, the apparition ordered me to obey it. I got up quietly, fearing that I would awaken someone—though there was none in that room! Most of the rooms of the palace used to remain shut and I never tried entering them. That night, I don't know where all I went!

Although I had not seen the apparition, yet I could picture her. She was an Arab with white hands peering through long, loose sleeves. She had a thin veil over her face and a twisted knife tied under her waistband. I felt I was in one of the thousand tales from the Arabian Nights! Finally, the apparition came and stood before a dark blue curtain and pointed down. There was nothing there but my blood curled with fear. I felt as if on the floor in front of the curtain, sat a *khoja* with a sword. The apparition stepped before me and went inside.

Inside, we saw a carpet. I could not see who was sitting on the *diwan*. The only thing I saw was beautiful feet in slippers made of *zari*, below snuff-coloured pyjamas. On a blue-coloured plate were kept a few apples, pears, oranges and lots and lots of bunches of grapes. There were two small cups and a golden decanter waiting for the guests. I could smell the intoxicating perfume of incense sticks.

With a trembling heart, as I tried to go over the *khoja's* feet, he woke up with a start and the sword fell to the ground with a thud.

Just then, I heard a loud scream. I sat up on the cot and looked up at the faint new moon. As usual, Meher Ali went about screaming on the empty road, asking people to move away. This is how I spent one Arabian Night. There were still a thousand nights remaining.

Every morning, I used to get up tired; go to do my work at the office and every evening, return home to the sleepless, cursed nights. My job now seemed lowly, illusionary and amusing. Every evening, I'd go back to the old ages and get enraptured by it. My shirt and my trousers did not suit that image any longer. I would throw away my cigarette, wear loose pyjamas, long kurtas and, with a perfumed handkerchief in my hand, sit on a high place with sausage cushions on my side; as if waiting for someone who had driven me mad. It was the same every night. I would not sleep but would roam from one room to another, looking for that beautiful apparition.

There were times when I'd sit before the mirror, trying to get ready, when I'd see the beautiful woman's reflection in the mirror, standing beside me and then, it would vanish. I could hear beautiful music, could feel her breath on my forehead and could feel her veil falling on my cheeks. She would attract me and soon, I'd fall off to sleep.

One day, I was trying to mount a horse to go riding. Someone was trying to forbid me to do so. She would not let me go. But, today, I did not listen to her. Suddenly, I saw a sand storm rise from near the Shusta river and close to the Aravalli Mountains. As I was about to pick up my *kurta* and my hat, the storm came and took them away. They could not be sighted anymore. I could not go for horse riding that day. And since then, I gave up wearing the long *kurta* and the hat.

Then, one night, I woke up to the sound of sobbing. The floor, the bed, the walls—the entire room seemed to echo the sound of sobbing—as if someone was weeping and telling me to take her out of that hell. I wondered how I could take her with me. I didn't even know who she was, where she came from and where she belonged to! I don't know who had taken her to be a part of his harem or to sell her in the marketplace. Just then, Meher Khan came in screaming, "Move away! Move away! Everything is a lie!" I looked up to see that it was morning. The peon came in with my letters and the cook came to ask what I wanted to eat.

I said, "No, I shall not live in this house any more." I picked up my baggage and moved into the office room. Karim Khan, the caretaker of the office, looked at me and laughed while I sat down to do my work. As evening started setting in, I felt I had to go somewhere; I had to meet someone. The secretary's advice did not affect me. My work and everything else seemed useless and meaningless.

I threw away the pen, closed the exercise book and ran out. I took a carriage and without any instructions, the carriage moved fast and soon came and stood before that hungry palace and I found myself inside the big room.

Everything was quiet today, as if the rooms were angry with me. I wanted to pick up an instrument and sing and call her and say that the person who had left her and run away had come back to her. She should do what she wanted with him and destroy him completely.

Suddenly, from above, two tear drops fell on my forehead. All of a sudden, I saw dense clouds rising from the Aravalli Mountains. There was a trembling in the water, ground and the sky. A hurricane came and started shaking the huge doors of the big rooms of the palace. There was none to light a lamp here as everyone was in the office room. I clearly saw a lady lying on the carpet. She was pulling at and tearing her hair. Blood was oozing out from her forehead. She would sometimes cry loudly and sometimes, laugh loudly and beat her breast. The rain water wet her body completely. It rained the whole night. I went from room to room trying to console and pacify the lady who was weeping bitterly but there was none there.

Then I heard Meher Ali, the mad man, running across, shouting, "Everything is a lie. Move away! Move away!" I noticed that the day was breaking. I suddenly realised that Meher Ali too, may have lived here once and had now turned mad. That's why he could not keep himself away from this stone monster and would come here, in rain or in sunshine, to fulfil his duty.

I ran to him and asked, "Meher Ali! What is a lie?" Without answering me, he pushed me aside and continued shouting, "Move away! Everything is an illusion, a lie"; probably to warn himself!

I ran to the office and asked Karim Khan to tell me everything openly. What he said was:

"There was a time when many unsatisfied passions used to take place there. It was because of the curse of every unfulfilled desire and heartburn, every stone, every slab of the palace hungered and thirsted for a living being. The moment they'd find one, they'd entice and lure him. Of those who had spent three nights in the palace, Meher Ali was the only one who could come out as a mad person and roam around here and there. The others had, until then, not been able to resist their temptation.

I asked him if there was no way by which I could escape them. The old man told me there was only one way but that was an extremely difficult one. "Before that, I have to tell you the story of the female Irani slave of that Gulbarg. Such an amazing and heart-rending incident has never taken place in this world."

Just then, the coolies came and told us that the train was coming. I said, "So early?" As I tied up my bedding, the train entered the platform. In the first class compartment of that train, I saw an Englishman who had just woken up from sleep. He pushed his head out and tried to read the name of the station. As he saw a co-passenger, he shouted out a greeting and took him inside his compartment. All the rest of us got into the second class compartment.

We never got to know who the *Babu* was. Hence, we never came to know the end of the story. I said that the story was his own creation. He had fooled us. There was no truth in the story.

With this argument, my relations with my theosophist relative snapped for life.

14

VICTORY AND DEFEAT

I

THE princess' name was Aparajita. Shekhar, Uday Narayan's court poet, had never seen her. But, the day he would write some new poem, he would sit in court and recite it so loudly before the king that its sound would travel inside, to the female folk. He would sometimes see her shadow and sometimes, hear the sound of her anklets. The poet had to spend his spare time there and set his songs to the tune and the beat of these anklets.

When Manjari, the princess' maid, used to go to the riverside, she had to pass Shekhar's room. She always exchanged pleasantries with him. When she'd find no one around, she would go inside Shekhar's room in the morning and evening. People would make fun of her and would gossip about her; however, Shekhar used to feel great pleasure talking to Manjari and he made no effort to hide it. He even called her Vasantamanjari. This talk reached the king's ears too. He was overjoyed. He'd show curiosity and Shekhar would join him.

The king would laugh and ask, "Does the bumblebee sing only in the king's court?"

The poet would reply, "No, it even partakes of the honey of the flower." Everyone would joke about it. Even Princess Aparajita would tease Manjari, but it did not upset her.

This is how a human life goes by—a little is created by God, a bit gets created by itself and a little is created by human beings. The fact that the poet would sing these songs, was the only truth and the complete thing—The theme?—The same—Radha and Krishna; of man and woman; of eternal sorrow and endless joy. His own story was written within these songs—everyone—from the king to the common man, would start introspecting. His songs were on everyone's lips. There was no limit to his fame.

A number of days went by. The poet used to write his poems, the king used to hear them, the courtiers applauded him, Manjari would come to the riverside and sometimes, a shadow used to fall from the inner rooms and sometimes, an anklet could be heard.

II

Just then a poet, roaring poetry in praise of the king, came into the king's court. He had come out of his state and after defeating the court poets of various other states, had finally come to Amrapur.

With great respect, the king said, "What do you want?"

The poet said, "War!"

Now, one had to save the king's honour. So, a war would have to be fought, but Shekhar did not have a very clear idea about how a poetic war would be fought. He became doubtful and worried. He couldn't sleep. He started seeing his solid body, sharp nose and tall frame all over the place.

In the morning, he entered the battlefield with a trembling heart. The hall was jam-packed. Smiling with great difficulty, Shekhar saluted the competitor—Poet Pundareek while the latter only indicated a salute and turning to his supporters, sniggered!

Shekhar turned his glance towards the inner rooms once and realised that hundreds of eyes were falling on him. He just prayed to the Goddess of victory and said (in his mind), "If I am victorious today, O Goddess! O Aparajita! Then it will bring significance to your name only!"

Trumpets were blowing. Everyone around stood up. King Uday Narayan, in spotless white clothes, entered the auditorium slowly and sat on the throne.

Pundareek came and stood in front of the throne and the court started. Pundareek started singing praises of the king in his deep, husky voice. It echoed not only in the Assembly Hall, the market place but also on the terrace, the seas—everywhere. Everyone was amazed at the innumerable words he used to draw a picture of King Uday Narayan. When Pundareek finally sat down, there was silence. Only his voice seemed to echo. Then scholars and all others started applauding him.

The king turned and looked at Shekhar's face. He too, looked at the king with respectful, devoted, loving and hesitant eyes. Then, he slowly stood up before the king, just as Sita did, when Ram wanted her to take the *Agni-Pareeksha*, as if trying to tell him, "I am yours only, but if you want to test me before the whole world, then do so, but..." He lowered his gaze.

Pundareek had stood like a tiger; Shekhar stood like a hunted deer! In a soft voice, he started reciting his poem. The people probably could not hear the first *shloka* (couplet). Then, slowly, he raised his face and as he spoke, the whole room seemed to resound with age-old history. He sang of the king's lineage (*Chandra vanshi*). Then, he sang of the wars, his valour, his sacrifices and came to the present and in poetry, expressed his subjects' devotion and love. Then, in the end he said, "O king! I can take defeat in words, but who can defeat me in your devotion?" And trembling, he sat down. Then, in tears, the public shouted, "Victory! Victory!"

Scorning the hysteria of the common public, Pundareek got up once again and asked, "Who or what is greater than speech?" For a moment, everyone became quiet. Then, with various words, he started proving that speech was the greatest; it was the truth and the *Brahma*. Brahma, Vishnu and Mahesh are all subservient to speech; hence it is greater than all the three. Brahma was unable to end speech even with his four mouths, while Panchanan was unable to end it with his five faces. Then he asked the same question again, "Who is greater in comparison to speech?"

When he got no reply, he took his seat once again, amidst accolades from the scholars. The king continued watching, aghast, while Shekhar considered himself much inferior. The assembly adjourned for the day.

III

The next day, Shekhar came and started singing—the flute first played in Vrindavan—and at that time, the *gopis* (girls of the village) did not know who played it, or where. Once they felt that it was calling them to meet their lover (Krishna), at another time, it seemed to cry because it had parted with its beloved. No one could understand what the flute said, but the heart longed for something.

Forgetting the assembly, the king himself, the opponent's fame and notoriety, victory and defeat, reply and counter-reply...everything, Shekhar stood alone and continued playing the flute. All he remembered was an illuminated lady; all he could hear was the sound of the two anklets. When the poet sat down after finishing the song, no one could preach anything. After a while Pundareek stood in front of the throne and said, "Who is Radha and who is Krishna?" Then he looked all around towards his pupils, laughed and then asked, the same question again. Then, he started giving a reply himself. He gave explanations for all the letters in Radha-Krishna; explained that if Krishna was the *yajna* (sacrifice), then Radha was the fire; then, said that if Radha was the problem, then Krishna was the solution. Then, he glanced at the king, at the scholars and finally, with a sharp, scornful snigger at Shekhar, Pundareek sat down.

The king was enamoured by Pundareek's surprising ability. Shekhar started considering his songs useless. After this, he did not have the capacity to sing and the assembly broke up.

IV

The next day, Pundareek exhibited his capacity to play with words. The songs that Shekhar used to write were in very simple language. Today, he could understand that it was not good—as if everyone and anyone could write it if he so desired; that his poems did not have anything new in them. He seemed an infant, an ordinary person in front of Pundareek.

Today was the last day—the day of decision—of victory and defeat. The king glanced at his court poet as if trying to say that he could not remain without a reply today and that he would have to try his best.

Shekhar stood up and said, "O Goddess with the *Veena* in your hands! If you leave your lotus and come and stand with us, we'll be able to defeat them all."

This made Pundareek laugh aloud. The scholars and all the other courtiers joined him, while the king kept glaring at him; but Shekhar did not care. This angered the king. He got off the throne, took off the pearl necklace from around his neck and put it around Pundareek's neck. Everyone in the court started applauding him.

When Shekhar heard the sound of innumerable bangles, he left his seat and walked out of the hall.

V

It was the night before the new moon. It was pitch dark. The south wind blew across the town. Shekhar had brought down his registers from the wooden platform and kept them in front of him. Then, he separated his own writings—some of which he had even forgotten. They also seemed worthless to him today.

He heaved a deep sigh and said, "Is this all that I have saved throughout my life?" There's no beauty, no joy, no music! Just as a sick person does not find any taste in the food he eats, he also threw away everything that came close to his hand. He tore off all his notebooks and threw them into the fire. Then, some thought struck him. He said to himself, "Famous kings have done sacrifices earlier. Today, I am making this sacrifice of my poems." Then, he felt that the comparison was not good because an *Ashwamedh* is performed when the horse returns undefeated. And he was doing the sacrifice the day his poetry had lost. He threw all his poetry into the fire and raising both his empty hands, said, "I gave it to you O! Beautiful fire, I gave it to you. I have given up everything. For a long time you burnt in my heart. If I had been made of gold, I would have become brighter, but I am worthless. That is why I have been born today."

It was late at night. Shekhar opened all the windows. He had gathered all the flowers that he loved—*Bela, Juhi* and *Gandharaj*. He scattered them on the bed and lit lamps in the room. Then, he mixed honey and poison, had it and slowly lay down on his bed. His body became senseless.

The sound of anklets was heard with drowsy eyes and the poet said, "Are you being kind to your devotee, O Goddess! After all these days, you have come to me today!" He heard a sweet voice answering, "Yes. I have come." Shekhar got up with a start and rubbed his eyes. He saw an extremely beautiful girl sitting on the bed. Then, she said, "I am Princess Aparajita." The poet sat up. The princess said, "The king did not do justice to you. You only have won. That is why I have come to put this garland of victory around your neck." And taking the garland made by her own hands from around her neck, Aparajita put it around the poet's neck. And the poet fell down on his bed.... Dead!

15

CHARITY AND COMPENSATION

WHAT the elder lady of the house said was both sharp and venomous. It upset the poor lady on whom she had showered those words—especially what she had said about her husband who had finished his meal and was now sitting and having betel a little away. It seemed that the statements had not had much effect on him. Not perturbed, he finished his betel, and as was his habit, went to sleep at the right time. But, this could not be expected of everyone. Today, Rashmoni came into the bedroom and behaved in a manner, as she had never done before this. Every day, she used to enter the room quietly and get down to pressing his legs; but, today, she straightaway came to lie down on the bed facing the other way.

Radhamukund did not pay much attention but, realising that his indifference was making his wife angrier, he let her know that since he'd have to wake up early in the morning for some work, hence it was essential that he slept.

On hearing her husband's voice, Rashmoni could not control her tears and said, "Did you not hear anything?" Radhamukund said, "Yes, I did hear. But sister-in-law did not tell a lie. Have I not been brought up by *dada*? All your clothes and jewellery etc.? Why? Have I bought it all with my money? If one who feeds and clothes us, says things like these, we have to take them with every morsel."

"Of what use are such food and clothes?"

"We have to live, to survive, don't we?"

"It would be better to die!"

"Let us try and sleep till that happens. We'll feel relaxed," said Radhamukund and went off to sleep.

He and Shashibhushan were not brothers. In fact, they were not too close either—they both belonged to the same village; but the love between them was no less than brothers. Brajsundari, the elder sister-in-law found it intolerable—especially because Shashibhusan treated his wife and his sister-in-law equally. In fact, if he did not find two similar things, he would first give it to Rashmoni. He used to depend more on the advice of Radhamukund than of his wife. He was also rather lazy, that is why he had to depend on Radhamukund to do his household chores. The elder sister-in-law always suspected that Radhamukund was exploiting his brother.

The next morning, Radhamukund went and stood seriously before Shashibhushan. The latter asked, "Why do you look like that, Radhe? I hope you are not unwell?" Radhamukund spoke softly, "*Dada,* I cannot live here any more." Then, he narrated all the aggressive statements that the elder sister-in-law had made the previous evening.

Shashibhushan laughed and said, "There's nothing new in it. She comes from another house and will say something or the other the moment she gets a chance. Does that mean that any member of the family will have to leave home and go away? Even I have to listen to things off and on but I cannot sacrifice my home!"

Radha said, "I cannot bear a woman's words or else, why was I born a man? The only thing I am scared of is, it will lead to unrest in your household."

Shashibhushan said, "How will your going solve my problems?" There was no more conversation. Radhamukund heaved a sigh and went away, but the weight on his heart remained.

The elder sister-in-law's anger, on the other hand, kept on rising. On thousands of occasions, she did not hesitate to say rude things to Radha; she practically killed Rashmoni's spirits.

Although Radha used to drag the hubble bubble very silently and would start snoring the moment he set eyes on his depressed wife, yet, he felt that it was getting intolerable for him.

His relation with Shashibhushan, however, were very old—those days, as children, when they used to bunk school, listen to stories, run away from home and watch theatre and get punished the next morning—where were Brajsundari and Rashmoni then?! How could he forget those days and go away? But, just then, an important incident took place.

One day, news was received that Shashibhushan's zamindari had been auctioned. In his natural soft way, Radhamukund said, "It was my fault."

Shashibhushan said, "How is it your fault? You had paid your dues. If the dacoits loot you, what can you do?"

It's no use deciding whose fault it was. Shashibhushan was not in the habit of taking on just any job. He felt as if he had fallen into a deep sea. At first, he decided to mortgage his wife's jewellery, but Radhamukund did not allow him to do that. He put a bagful of money before Shashibhushan. He had already mortgaged his wife's jewellery and collected all this money.

A great change was noticed in the family. The lady of the house was trying to hold on to the person she had once wanted to throw away when they were prosperous. She did not take long to understand who she could depend on. The hatred she had for Radhamukund once, was not visible today.

Radhamukund had been prepared to earn an independent income. He started working as an attorney in a close city. With his intelligence, Radhamukund soon established himself. Slowly, he took on the responsibility of the majority of the district's zamindars.

Rashmoni's condition was right the opposite of what it was earlier. Now it was she and her husband who were taking care of Shashibhushan and his wife. One does not know if she was proud of this fact or not, but one day, she had, through her action and behaviour, became even more humble than before. This was so because she came to know that her husband had planned to send her back to her parents' house and had not seen her face for a week. Finally Brajsundari had pleaded with her brother-in-law, saying, "The young girl came into our family just the other day, while I have been there for ages. She will take time to learn to value our sweet relationship. Forgive her for she is young."

Radhamukund would give all the money for household expenses to Brajsundari. Rashmoni would have to ask her for money for her expenses. Within the house, the elder sister-in-law's condition was better than before.

Although Shashibhushan would be smiling all the time, yet, day-by-day, he was becoming physically weak. No one observed this except Radha. He could not sleep. Many times, Rashmoni would wake up in the middle of the night, to see Radha tossing and turning. Often, he would go to his elder brother and say, "Don't worry *dada.* I shall soon pay and bring back all the ancestral property. I shall not let it go, and it shall not be too long either." And it really did not take long. The person who had bought all the property was a trader, who did not know anything about *zamindari.* Once or twice a year, Radhamukund would take miscreants with him and collect the revenue. The man became anxious to get rid of the property and Radhamukund bought it for a measly amount.

About ten years had passed. Shashibhushan had become old. Probably because of that, he was not so excited when he got back the property. The people of the village wanted to express their joy. So, they asked for a treat. Shashibhushan asked Radha, who said, "Definitely."

Such a treat had never been given in this village. Everyone enjoyed the feast. The Brahmins and the poor received money and clothes. They blessed them and went away.

The village was facing bad times at the beginning of winters. Shashibhushan had worked a lot and his weak body could not tolerate it any more—he became bed-ridden. Besides other ailments, he also developed very high fever. In the middle of the night, Radhamukund sent everyone out of the room and said,

"*Dada*, when you are not there, who shall I give your share of the property to?"

Shashibhushan said, "What is mine that I should think of who to give it to? I had property once, but now I don't."

For a long time, Radhamukund sat quietly. Then, he got up, held both his brother's feet and said, "*Dada*, I have committed a grave crime. Let me tell you that now; now that there's no time."

Shashibhushan did not give any reply. Radhamukund said, "I do not have the capacity to say it properly. Right from our childhood, we had no differences between us except that you were rich and I was poor. When I saw that the possibility of us parting was becoming great, I took advantage of it. I had the government exchequer looted and got your property auctioned."

Without showing any surprise, Shashibhushan laughed and said, "I am glad you did that, brother. But were you able to achieve what you tried to achieve? Were you able to keep it close to you?" Two tears fell from Radhamukund's eyes and he said, "Have you forgiven me, *Dada?*"

Shashibhushan called him close and holding his hand, said, "Listen, I knew it all along. Those with whom you had conspired had come and confided in me. I had forgiven you then only."

Radhamukund covered his face and crying, said, "If you have forgiven me, then please accept your property and do not return it in anger."

Shashibhushan could not give any reply—he only raised his right hand. Probably Radhamukund understood its meaning.

16

THE EDITOR

I had no worry for Prabha—I used to be satisfied with Prabha's games, her talks and her love. I played with her as long as I wanted and gave her in her mother's lap as soon as she'd start crying. I never realised that I would have to bring her up with great difficulty.

Finally, with my wife's untimely death, the child fell into my lap. I could not understand whether I was more worried about that fact that it was now my duty to raise her and give her the love of both, a father and a mother or whether she was more worried that it was now her duty to take great care of her widowed father! But, she had started behaving like the lady of the house from the young age of six years...And I had, laughingly, surrendered myself into her hands. I realised that she liked it a lot when I pretended to be helpless. She would get angry if I took my clothes or the umbrella myself—as if I was interfering with her rights. She had probably never handled as big a doll as her father!

I realised that I would need a lot of money at the time of her marriage, but where was the money? Besides, I was trying to give her as much education as I could. What if she finally landed up in the hands of a fool?!

I had crossed the age of working in a government office. I did not have the ability to join elsewhere. So finally, I decided to write a book. It was staged as a play and was an instant success.

The taste of success was so good that I could not stop myself from writing.

Prabha, my daughter, came and said, "*Baba*, won't you go in for a bath?" I just snubbed her and asked her to leave the room. The poor girl went out sadly. I scolded the maids and even those passers-by who asked me the way—I'd ask them to go to hell!

I got lots of fame but not as much money. It did not affect me then. I even forgot about finding a groom for Prabha. Just then, a *zamindar* of Jahirgram sent a request to me. He was planning to bring out a paper and wanted me to become the Editor of that paper. I accepted the offer.

Close to Jahirgram is Aahirgram. Both the zamindars were competitors. Earlier they used to get down to fighting at the slightest excuse. Now because of my writings, the *zamindar* of Aahirgram could not lift his head.

By now, I had put on weight and always had a smiling face. I used to write about the predecessors of Aahirgram and the people of Jahirgram were in splits of laughter.

Finally, the *zamindar* of Aahirgram also brought out a paper. It never used to keep anything secret. They used to abuse in such a language that it could be understood by all—whereas I was subtle.

The result was that although I had won, everyone thought I had lost. My master did not respect me as before; even people stopped coming to get acquainted with me. In fact, some people even used to start laughing at me when they saw me. I felt like a matchstick, which had burnt right till the end. I could not concentrate any more. I could not write even one line and I felt that there was no fun in living.

Prabha used to feel scared of me now. She did not have the courage to come close to me.

One day, I noticed that the paper of Aahirgram had stopped writing about our *zamindar* and had started writing horrible things about me. My close friends would take the paper and laugh and tell me about it. Some said, "Doesn't matter what the subject may be but its language is great!"

We had a little garden in front of our house. One day, I was strolling, all alone, with a heavy heart, over there. I sat and pondered over what reply I could give. One problem with decency is that all the persons cannot understand it whereas the language of indecency is better known. I decided that I would answer in that language only. I cannot take defeat! Just then, in the greyness of the dusk, I heard a familiar sound and felt a soft, warm touch.

The girl had come close and was calling out to me, "*Baba.*" Not getting any reply, she had held my left hand, rubbed it on her forehead and was now going back. For a long time now, Prabha had not called out to me like this.

After some time, I returned home and saw Prabha lying in bed. I touched her forehead. It was very hot. I realised that the little girl had gone to her father for a little attention, a little affection, whereas the father was thinking of giving a strong reply to Jahir Prakash.

I came and sat down. My little girl caught my hands and put them on her forehead and lay down quietly. I burnt all the papers of Aahirgram and Jahirgram. No reply was written. I never felt such happiness in accepting defeat. When the girl's mother had died, I had taken the girl in my lap. Today, once again, I embraced her and went into the room.

17

ELDER SISTER

I

IN very short, the neighbours of one unfortunate lady of Palli, expressed their views about her unjust, cruel husband by saying, "May such a husband be burnt."

When Jaigopal Babu's wife, Shashi heard this, she was very upset. According to her, no husband should experience any fire except that of a cigar, in his mouth. When she expressed her hesitation, these hard-hearted ladies said with double vengeance, "It is better to be widowed in seven lives rather than have a husband of this sort." The meeting was adjourned and everyone went their way.

In her mind, Shashi said, "I cannot imagine the husband committing such a crime for which one can have such strong feelings and think of giving such a punishment." With such thoughts in her mind, she went to her bedroom and caressing the pillow on the side of her husband's bed, got up, closed the door and taking a photograph and some letters written by her husband, went out. The day passed like this only.

It's not that Shashikala and Jaigopal had been recently married. They had had a child marriage, had had children and had spent their lives comfortably together. Now, when her husband was not there, she was miserable. She decided that she would not permit her life to be lifeless when she met her husband this time. She had argued with him and shown her temper many times. She now decided that she would not behave this way ever again. She would tolerate his temper for her husband was everything for her—her love and her god.

For a very long time, Shashikala was the only daughter of her parents. That is why, although Jaigopal had a very ordinary job, yet, he did not have any worry about his future. His father-in-law had enough property in Palligram for him to live like a king.

Just then, in their old age, Shashi's parents had a son. Shashi was very upset about the birth of child. Even Jaigopal was not very happy.

When this son, born in old age, took Jaigopal's hopes of getting wealth, Jaigopal took up a job in a tea estate in Assam. He left Shashi and the children in her father's house and went away. This was the first time that the two had separated. Because of this, Shashi was very angry with her little brother. She found some excuse or the other to create unpleasantness at home. The baby was still small when its mother passed away, leaving him to the care of his sister.

Shashi could not fight back against her toothless brother when he'd try and take her finger, cheek, nose—everything into his mouth, when he'd hold a bunch of her hair in his fist, when he'd wake up early in the morning and demand her attention, when he'd eat the forbidden food and go to forbidden places. So, she finally surrendered. He had more rights over because he did not have a mother.

II

The child was named Neelmoni. When he was two years old, his father had a severe attack of pain. Jaigopal was asked to come as soon as possible. By the time he arrived, his father-in-law was on his deathbed. Handing the child over to him, Kaliprasanna, Shashi's father, gave one-fourth of his property to his daughter. As a result, Jaigopal had to give up his job to come and take care of the property.

After a long time, the husband and the wife met. Shashi felt as if she had just remarried her husband. She swore to herself that whatever might happen, she would not allow her love for her husband to diminish; but Jaigopal was not the same. He felt that his wife had changed. A small infant, who was a total stranger to him, had taken control of her attention. She tried her best to bring the baby close to her husband, but one can't say whether she succeeded or not. Whenever Shashi would hold Neelmoni in front of her husband, the child would hide his face under her *sari*—not making the least effort to get into the formalities. Her husband too, could not understand what there was in this child, for him to get attracted to!

Shashi, like any other woman would, understood very quickly that Jaigopal did not have much love for her brother. She'd try to keep Neelmoni away from her husband. Slowly, the child became a thing for her love only. Everyone knows how intense a secret love becomes.

Jaigopal would get extremely irritated when Neelmoni cried. So, Shashi would immediately hold the child close to her heart, to make it stop crying, especially during the night.

When there was a fight between her sons and her brother, Shashi would take her brother's side and punish her sons—only because he did not have a mother. Now with the change in the judge, there was a change in the mode of punishment too. Now, although he was not at fault, Neelmoni was given severe punishment. This was intolerable for Shashi. So, she'd bring her brother into the room, give him toys, sweets, love and would try and soothe him.

The result of this was that the more Shashi loved Neelmoni, the more her husband would get irritated with him.

Jaigopal had never been harsh with his wife.

III

Neelmoni's head was a large one. Doctors had also expressed their apprehensions that the boy would not live long—he'd grow like a bubble and then blow up. He could not speak or walk for a very long time. Seeing his serious face, one would feel that his aged parents had put all their old age problems and stress on his shoulders. With his sister's love and care, Neelmoni grew up to be six years old.

It was the month of *Kartik* (October-November). The day was *Bhai-Duj* (The second day of the new moon. It is celebrated as a day for brothers). Shashi had dressed Neelmoni up in a red bordered white *dhoti* and a new shirt and was about to put the red mark on his forehead, when her neighbour, who used to speak rudely, came and under one pretext or the other, started a fight with her. She said that Shashi had ruined her brother's life and was now pretending by putting the red mark on his forehead. That the husband and the wife had conspired and auctioned all Neelmoni's property; and bought it all off in the name of his cousin.

Not being able to control her anger, Shashi cursed her. Then, weeping, she went to her husband and told him about it.

Jaigopal said, "In today's time, one can't trust anyone. I had given my cousin the job of taking care of the property. God knows when he bought it all off!"

Amazed, Shashi asked, "Are you not going to complain?"

Jaigopal said, "How do I complain against my own cousin? Besides, complaining does not yield any results. It only adds on to the expenses."

It was Shashi's basic duty to trust her husband, but she could not. What she had until now, considered to be her refuge, turned out to be a cruel place—it had enclosed the brother and the sister from all sides. How she, a lone lady, would be able to protect her brother, she did not seem to understand. The more she worried about it, the more love she felt for her brother. She felt that if she could, she'd go to the Lord or the Queen and request them to protect her brother's property. The queen would never allow her brother's property to be sold off. Just when Shashi was thinking of doing so, Neelmoni suddenly developed very high temperature and started getting convulsions. Jaigopal called a native doctor. When Shashi requested him to get a good doctor, he said, "Why, is Motilal a bad doctor?"

Shashi sat the whole day, with Neelmoni on her lap. Even Neelmoni did not leave her for a minute; even while he slept, he kept holding on to one end of her *sari.* The whole day passed. In the evening, Jaigopal came and said that he had not been able to meet the doctor in the city as he had gone to see a patient far away. He further said that he would have to go elsewhere in connection with a case and that he had told Motilal to come and check the patient regularly.

At night, Neelmoni started muttering in his sleep. At dawn, Shashi, without a second thought, took her brother in her lap, climbed on to a boat and presented herself at the house of the doctor in the city. The doctor was at home only and had not gone out of the city. Seeing a lady, he got up quickly and making Shashi sit down, started examining the patient.

Jaigopal came to the city the next day itself. Burning with anger, he ordered his wife to immediately return with him. The wife said, "I shall not return just now, even if you kill me. You want to kill my Neelmoni. He doesn't have a father, or a mother. He has no one except me and I shall protect him."

Angrily, Jaigopal said, "In that case, you stay here only and never return to my house."

Shashi answered, "What do you mean by 'your house'? The house belongs to my brother."

For a few days, the people of the neighbourhood revolted against this. Tara, a neighbour, said, "Why don't you stay at home and fight with your husband?"

Shashi sold off all her jewellery and spent all the money she had. She was finally able to pull her brother out of the jaws of death. It was then that she got the news that Jaigopal had transferred their house in Dwarigram into his name. Now nothing belonged to her brother.

Weak from the illness, Neelmoni said, "*Didi* let's go home." Shashi knew that he was missing his nieces and nephews, but she could do nothing except cry, as now, they did not have any house of their own. Then she realised that it was pointless to cry. Her brother had no one to fight on his behalf, except her. So, she went to meet the wife of Tarini *babu*, the Deputy Magistrate. Tarini *babu* knew Jaigopal. He got a little irritated with Shashi for wanting to enter into a dispute with her husband. He wrote a letter to Jaigopal who came and forcibly took his wife and brother-in-law back home, in a boat.

Neelmoni was thrilled to come back home.

IV

During the winters, the magistrate *saheb* pitched a tent for a hunt in the village. On the way to the village, Neelmoni met the *saheb*. Seeing the magistrate, the other children moved away, but the serious Neelmoni stood and examined the *saheb* with curiosity. *Saheb* came and asked him, "Do you study in school?" The child nodded his head and said, "Yes." The *saheb* asked, "Which book have you read?" Not understanding the meaning of the word 'book', he kept staring at the face of the magistrate.

On his return home, he narrated his meeting with the magistrate to his sister.

The magistrate sat inside the tent and was asking Jaigopal about the local conditions. Just then, a lady came in with Neelmoni and stood before the tent gate and said, "*Saheb,* I am handing over this orphan brother of mine into your hands. Please protect him."

Saheb recognised the boy and seeing a lady before him, stood up and said, "Please come in." The lady said, "I shall say whatever I have to say, here only." The people of the village started collecting all around. Meanwhile, Shashi narrated the entire history of the orphaned boy. When Jaigopal tried to hinder her speech, the magistrate, with a red face, would scream, "Be quiet." Then, he ordered him to leave his seat and come and stand before him. Neelmoni stood very close to his sister and kept listening, astonished.

The magistrate then asked Jaigopal a few questions. After hearing his reply, he sat silently for some time and then addressing Shashi, said, "Although I cannot take up this case right now, you can rest assured that I shall do what I can in connection with this case. You may return home with your brother."

Shashi said, "*Saheb*, till such time that I do not get back our house, I do not have the courage to take my brother's home. Now, no one can protect him unless you keep him in your house."

Saheb said, "And where will you go?"

Shashi said, "I shall return to my husband's house. I do not have any fear." *Saheb* agreed to take the boy with him. When the boy saw his sister going, he held on to her *sari.* The *saheb* called him. Shashi, weeping, told him to go with the assurance that she'd see him again.

She met her husband again but it did not last for long because within a few days, it was heard that Shashi had died and at night only, she had been cremated. No one said anything except the neighbourhood lady, but she was made to be quiet. God knows whether Shashi was able to fulfil her promise to her brother.

18

GRANDFATHER

THE zamindars of Nayanjorh were once famous as babus. At that time, their ideals were not so easy. Just as one has to go through a lot of rituals if one wants the title of *Raja* or *Rai Bahadur*, at that time, getting to be called a *babu* was just as tough. They used to wear *Dhakai* dhotis because the bordered dhotis used to hurt their delicate legs. They used to spend lakhs on the wedding of their cats. Hence, everyone can understand that this style could not be maintained for generations to come.

Our Kailash Chandra Rai Chaudhary was a *babu* of this famous place. At the time when he was born, there was huge property left for him. In fulfilling a few of the extraordinary rituals of their family, the last of his property was sold off to pay the debts. Whatever little was left was not enough to protect the fame of the ancestors.

Hence, Kailash *babu* gave up Nayanjorh and taking his son, came to settle down in Kolkata. Then, leaving his son and a daughter, he left this earth for his heavenly abode.

We are his neighbours in Kolkata. Our history was totally the opposite of theirs. My father has earned totally through his own efforts; he never wore his *dhoti* below his knees, was very strict about the accounts and had no desire to be called a *babu.* Therefore I, his one and only son, am grateful to him. The fact that I have received education and have acquired property to protect my prestige without much effort, is enough for me. I preferred to have the papers of our ancestral property in my possession, rather than the glowing history of ancestral babus.

I suppose it was because of this that when Kailash *babu* used to draw cheques on their old, failed bank for huge amounts, it seemed intolerable to me. It seemed as if he was trying to show his hatred for us because my father had earned everything with his own hands. I used to get angry and wonder who was worthy of this hatred?

I was young then—that is why I used to argue and get angry. I am old now. Now, I feel—what was the harm in it? I have enough property and no scarcity. If a person, who has no money, feels happy in his vanity, it doesn't harm me at all!

It has also been seen that nobody, besides me, used to be angry with Kailash *babu* because such a great man is seldom seen. He always cooperated with his neighbours. He used to ask about the welfare of everyone—whether he was a youth or an old man. That is why a regular question-answer session used to start when he met anyone. He was an extremely neat and clean person. He didn't have many clothes, but he was always well-dressed. The *Mirzai* shawl was gorgeous. He used to sun his bedsheet, pillow, the *durrie* etc. and fold it meticulously. He had lost most of his property, but had, with great efforts, been able to secure an expensive *golabapaas, itrdaan*, a golden plate and an expensive shawl. On any occasion, all these were brought out.

Although he was a simpleton, yet, vanity used to be reflected in his talks. Everyone used to encourage him and he felt thrilled. They used to call him *Thakurdamoshai* and used to generally gather at his house. So that he may not feel the scarcity, someone or the other of the neighbourhood used to bring a kg of tobacco before him and say, "*Thakurdamoshai*, please try this. It is good tobacco from Gaya."

Thakurdamoshai used to take one or two puffs and say, "It's really good!" And, he used to start talking about expensive tobacco and ask if anyone desired to smoke that tobacco. Everyone knew that if they expressed the desire to taste it, then the key would not be found, or the blame would fall on Ganesha, who would gladly take the blame. That is why, everyone used to unanimously say, "No *Thakurdamoshai*, it's not required. We won't be able to digest it. This one is okay for us." *Thakurdamoshai* would only laugh. When they were about to leave, he'd shout, "Alright, tell me when you all will eat here." And everyone used to say, "We'll decide on a day." He'd say, "Correct! Let the rains come and the temperature fall or else there's no good food in this heat." And no one used to remind *Thakurdamoshai* of his promise even when it rained. In fact, if talks of a meal started, they'd say, "It won't be comfortable till the rain stops."

Everyone accepted that this was too small a house for him to live in, yet, they could not deny that it was very difficult to buy a house in Kolkata. Ultimately, *Thakurdamoshai* used to say, "Leave it. I'm very happy to stay close to you. We have a big house in Nayanjorh, lying empty, but I do not like living there."

I feel, even *Thakurda* knew that everyone knew his condition and when he pretended that the old Nayanjorh was modern and when everyone else agreed to it, then, he used to understand that all this was because of mutual love between them. However, I used to feel irritated. Kailash *babu* was not so innocent. Everyone used to consult him in their work.

Sometimes I felt like publicly blowing up the castle that he used to build in midair. As far as I can remember, there was another solid reason for my malice for Kailash *babu*. Although I belonged to an affluent family, I had done my M.A. at the right time; I did not get involved in any bad company or enjoyment and although I became the head of the family after my father's death, yet, it did not bring about any change in my nature. I knew that I had a very high price in the market and I swore that I would get it. A rich man's beautiful, educated daughter became my imaginary partner. From various places, I started getting offers, but I'd weigh their capabilities. No one seemed fit enough for me. Ultimately, I came to the conclusion that there may be someone equal to me; that there was enough time. But, I do not know if that impossible person had been born in Bengal or not.

Parents of various girls started worshipping me. Whether I liked the girl or not was different, but I did certainly enjoy this worshipping. At the very beginning, I had said that *Thakurdamoshai* also had a granddaughter. I had seen her many times, but never considered her beautiful. Hence, I never thought of marrying her, but in my mind, I had decided that Kailash *babu* will certainly come to ask me—either himself or through someone. But, that never happened. I heard that he had told my friend that the babus of Nayanjorh had never taken the initiative in any matter and gone with prayers to someone. He would not be able to break the system, even if it meant that the girl remained a spinster.

This really angered me, but I remained quiet because I was a good boy. I did not want to upset the old man, but one day I had a plan and I could not control myself. I have already said that many people used to tell many lies to please the old man. An old pensioner, a Deputy Magistrate, often used to say, "*Thakurda*, whenever I meet the Lord, he does not leave me without asking me about the babus of Nayanjorh. He always says that there are only two well established families here—family of the king of Burdwan and the babus of Nayanjorh."

This used to please *Thakurda* a great deal and whenever he met the former deputy *babu*, besides asking him of his welfare, he used to ask, "Is the Lord *Saheb* fine? How about his wife? I hope their children too are fine." He also expressed a desire to go and meet the *Saheb* soon. However, the former deputy definitely knew that by time the Chaudharys of Nayanjorh come and meet the Lord, they would have changed or replaced each other.

One day, I called Kailash *babu* aside and whispered, "*Thakurda*, I went to the Lt. Governor's lobby last night. When he spoke of the babus of Nayanjorh, I told him that you were in Kolkata itself. When he heard this, he expressed his sorrow at not being able to come and see you. He said that he would secretly come to see you this afternoon itself."

Had it been about anyone else, he would have understood the impossibility of what I had said, but because it was concerning him, he did not mistrust it even one bit. He was as anxious as he was thrilled—where will he be seated, what will have to be done, how would he be able to protect the glory of Nayanjorh—he could not decide.

I said, "I am not worried about that. A translator stays with him, but the Assistant Lord desires that no one else should be present."

When in the afternoon, majority of the people had gone to office and the rest were sleeping with their doors shut, a carriage came and stood in front of Kailash babu's house. The peon came and gave him the news that the Lord *Saheb* had come. *Thakurda* was ready and so was his relative, Ganesha. On hearing that the Lord *Saheb* had come, he ran to the door, panting and saluting him many times, took my dear old friend, dressed as an Englishman, into the room. He had covered a stool with his expensive shawl. He made the Lord *Saheb* sit on it and in chaste Urdu recited a long welcome speech. Then, in his hand he had a golden plate with a necklace of gold coins which had been protected for generations with great difficulty.

Ganesha came in with the *golabapaash* and the *itrdaan*.

Time and again, Kailash *babu* continued repeating that if *Saheb* Bahadur had visited his Nayanjorh's house, then he could have organised an appropriate welcome. He was a migrant here. My friend, with a long hat on his head, started nodding very seriously.

According to English custom, the hat was supposed to be off, but my friend, for the fear of getting caught, did not take it off. Anyone, except Kailash *babu* and his foolish friend, would have caught on to it.

After ten minutes, my friend got up and as per the lesson given to them, the peons collected the golden plate, the gold coin necklace, the shawl, the *golabapaash* and the *itrdaan* and took it into the car. Kailash *babu* thought this was the Lord's custom. I was hiding in the neighbouring room and watching all this. My ribs were about to burst because I was controlling my laughter. Finally, I couldn't take it any more. I ran to a neighbouring room, laughed my heart out and relieved myself. Then, I saw a girl lying on her stomach on top of a *diwan*, weeping bitterly. Seeing me enter the room laughing, she got up and staring at me, shouted, "What wrong has my grandfather done to you? Why have you come to deceive him? Why?"

She couldn't think of anything else to say, so, covering her face, she burst out crying.

My laughter died! I did not realise that until now that what I had done had nothing but curiosity—I suddenly felt that I had given a very hard blow at a very soft spot! My misdeed glared at me. Shamefully, I came out of the room. True—what wrong had the old man done? His useless conceit had never hurt any person, then why did mine do so?

Besides this, I realised something else too. Until now, I used to consider Kusum as a product, waiting for the glance of some bachelor—I thought that she was still unmarried because I did not like her. Today, I realised that she too was a human being. Was she really the kind who could be selected or chosen only because of her looks or her property?

I couldn't sleep the whole night. The next day, I went stealthily to Thakurda's house with all the expensive things I had taken—I had thought I'd hand over everything to the servant and come away without saying anything to anyone. Not finding the servant anywhere, I was wondering what to do when I heard the girl sweetly talking to the old man. She was asking him, "*Dadamoshai*, what did the Lord *Saheb* say to you yesterday?" Very happily, *Thakurda* was translating all the imaginary words spoken by the Lord *Saheb* in praise of the family of Nayanjorh. The girl showed curiosity at it. Seeing this small motherly girl comfort the old man with deceit brought tears to my eyes. I kept sitting quietly for a long time. Finally, when *Thakurda* went away after finishing his story, I went to the girl with all the things taken the previous day, kept them in front of her without a word and came away.

As per today's custom, I would not have said anything to the old man the next day when I saw him, but I saluted him. He must have thought this was because the Lord *Saheb* had visited him the previous day. He was thrilled and started making up stories of the Lord's visit to his house. I also did not contradict him but played along. When the others had left, I made a proposal, "Although our lineage cannot be compared to that of the babus of Nayanjorh, yet..." As soon as the proposal ended, the old man embraced me and said, "I am poor—that my fate shall be so good, I did not know—my Kusum must have done a number of good deeds. That is why I have got you today." And he started crying.

This was the first time that the old man had forgotten to safeguard his ancestor's glory and had accepted that he was poor.

19

MONIHARA

MY boat had been harboured on the side of Bandhaghat. The sun had set. The boatman was sitting on top of the boat, reading his *namaaz*.

I was sitting all alone in the verandah which had a broken window, admiring the beautiful scene when I was suddenly shaken up by someone's voice asking, "Where are you coming from, Sir?"

I looked up and saw an extremely thin, nearly famished man standing there. He sat down next to me. I said, "I have come from Ranchi."

"What do you do there?" the man asked.

"Business," I replied.

"What business?" he again asked.

"I deal in silk and wood," I answered.

And then, he asked two more questions. "What is your name? Why have you come here?" I gave him some name, not my own and said, "Change of place."

He seemed surprised. He said, "Sir, for the past nearly six years, I have been enjoying the climate and also taking 15 grains of quinine every day, but have had no results."

I said, "You'll have to agree the atmosphere here is very different to that in Ranchi." He said, "Where will you put up?" I pointed to the dilapidated house above the banks and said, "There."

The man probably suspected that I had gone there for some

secret hidden property, but he did not put up any argument in this regard. He just narrated, in detail, about the incident that took place 15 years ago, in this cursed house. The school master said:

About ten years before I came to this village, Phanibhushan Saha used to live in this house. He had inherited all the property and the business of Durga Mohan. He had learnt to read and write. He could go into the Sahib's office with his shoes on and could speak proper English. Besides, he had kept a beard. Hence, there was no possibility of his getting a promotion with his Sahib merchant. He looked every inch, a modern Bengali.

At home too, there was a problem. His wife was very beautiful and had studied in college. Hence, her behaviour and actions were not as per the times. To the extent that if she fell ill, the Assistant Surgeon would be called.

Every married person knows that a woman likes raw mangoes, spicy chillies and a stern husband! The unfortunate man, who is deprived of his wife's love, is not poor but extremely helpless.

One is not happy until one's nature or capability is not discussed. A woman can, in various ways, entice a man. A woman, whose husband comes under her control by himself, is a poor soul, for all the knowledge of enticing a man that she had acquired, is of no use.

Phanibhushan's wife, Manimalika, had got all the love without trying for it; got a *Dhakai sari* without having to shed tears for it and got an armlet too the same way. Hence, her womanly nature and her love, along with it, had become lifeless. She only used to accept, not give anything. Her innocent husband used to feel that giving was probably the only way of receiving. Obviously, she had understood right the opposite.

Phanibhushan was born in Phulbere, which is a business centre. He had to spend most of his time there because of his job. He did not have mother but his maternal and paternal aunts etc., were there. It was probably for these aunts only that he had not brought his beautiful wife home. That is why he had brought her to this house and kept her alone with him.

His wife was not very talkative, nor did she mix around much with the women of the locality. She could never get herself to fast or to give charity to Brahmins or anyone else. Nothing ever got destroyed by her hand. Except for her husband's love, she had collected everything that she had got. She did not even allow her youth to decrease. People say, she looked like a 14-year old even at the age of 24 years. It seems, probably, that one who has a cold heart, one who does not feel love, remains fresh and young for a long time.

Unfortunately, the Creator did not give her a child, that is to say, He did not give her anything which she could value more than the jewels locked in her iron trunk. However, Manimalika was very tough as far as her work was concerned. She did not ever have much help at home. She could not tolerate the fact that someone else would take away money for the work that she could do. She did not worry about anyone; did not love anyone. All she did was work and collect wealth. That is why she did not suffer from any disease or sorrow.

For most husbands, this was enough or more than enough. A house runs on the husband doing his work and the wife doing hers—but God did give man the understanding; though in fact, there was no need for it. A man's love is a woman's strength and the main wealth. That is why God has given a woman the scale to measure love, not to man. But, man has, somehow, acquired it—thanks to the poets. I do not blame God. He has made the woman and the man quite different from each other. However, that difference has ceased to exist. A woman is trying to be a man and vice-versa. Hence, peace and order has gone out of every household.

Phanibhushan's wife did not have any fault or illusion. Yet, she did not have the pleasure of having a husband. All he did was get ornaments of pearls and diamonds and gift them to her; but they fell in the iron bore and her heart was always empty.

Uncle Durga Mohan did not understand love so minutely. He did not give so much but he used to receive a lot from his wife.

Just then, I heard an extremely loud scream of jackals from the nearby jungles. Master Moshai's flow of stories was disturbed for a while. When the howling stopped, Master *Moshai* opened his large eyes and started narrating the story:

Difficulty arose in the huge and complex business of Phanibhushan. For a non-businessman like me, it is difficult to understand and even explain the matter. One didn't understand how it became difficult for him to get credit in the market. If, within five days, he could somehow, manage to bring out one-and-a-half lakh rupees, if he could let the people in the market know he had it, then only could his business survive this calamity; but he was not being able to arrange it. If he borrowed it from known moneylenders, and if people got to know of it, then his business would suffer even more. So, he planned to take the money from unknown people; but here, he would have to mortgage something. If he mortgaged the jewellery, it would not take such a long time.

So, Phanibhushan went to his wife although he did not have the guts to do so. He could not say clearly, "I need it, please give me your jewellery." He said it but very weakly. However, when Manimalika did not give any reply, he was very hurt but did not respond that way because he was not barbaric as any other man would have been. Where he could actually snatch it from, he actually covered up his feelings. He could not force his wife if she did not want to give her jewellery. Keeping his pride, Phanibhushan did not touch his wife's jewellery but decided to go to Kolkata to find other ways of collecting money.

Generally, a wife understands her husband much more than he understands her but, Phanibhushan's wife did not understand him. She called her minister for advice. One of her cousins used to work under the caretaker of Phanibhushan's house. For some reason or the other, he used to get a salary and some more money, which he used to collect. Manimalika called him and told him everything, then said, "What do you advice?"

He shook his head like an intelligent man to say that it was not right. He said, "Sir will never be able to collect the money.

Ultimately, your jewellery will go." She became worried. She didn't have any children. The only thing she could claim as her own was the jewellery. She could not let it go so easily.

Madhusudan, the cousin, said, "Take your jewellery to your father's house." Madhusudan had already planned how to get some or most of his cousin's jewellery. Manimalika was not able to understand this, so she immediately agreed to this proposal.

On one evening at the end of *Aashaadh* (June), a boat lay at anchor in the harbour near the bank of the river. In the quiet darkness, Manimalika covered herself up with a thick sheet and got on to the boat. Madhusudan, who was sleeping in the boat, woke up and said, "Give the jewellery box to me." Mani said, "Later. Now, untie the boat." Madhusudan did that. The oars sank deep into the water. The whole night, Manimalika continued wearing all her jewellery. She did so because she thought that if she put the jewellery in a box, she might lose the box along with the jewellery in it. She felt that if she wore them, her jewellery would be safe as one would have to kill her to take it.

Not seeing any box with her, Madhusudan was worried because he did not understand anything. He did not realise that she could have worn the jewellery which she loved more than her life. Manimalika understood what Madhusudan was feeling. She had not been able to understand her husband but she understood Madhusudan through and through.

Madhusudan had left a letter with the caretaker to say that he was accompanying the lady of the house to her parents' home. The caretaker had been working here since the time of Phanibhushan's father. So, he wrote a letter to his master in broken *Bangla* in which he expressed his feelings that it was not right for a man to spoil or pamper his wife so much.

Phanibhushan understood Manimalika's feelings. He was greatly upset by the fact that although he was in deep financial trouble, he had not taken her jewellery and had come away to collect money from elsewhere. Yet, she suspected him! She had still not understood him!

Phanibhushan should have been angry at the disrespect that

was shown to him but he was not. God had made man to get angry at small instances and the woman to cry at the smallest of things but it did not happen that way.

Thinking about his defaulter wife, Phanibhushan said in his mind, "If that is your justice then let it be so. I shall continue doing my duty." Phanibhushan should have been born five or six centuries later. Unfortunately he was born in the nineteenth century, yet, had got married to a girl from the ancient times. He did not write even one letter to his wife and swore that he would never mention it to his wife.

After ten days, Phanibhushan had collected the required amount, so he returned home. Thinking that his wife would feel sorry and apologise for her behaviour, Phanibhushan came and stood near the room. He saw that the room was shut. He broke open the lock and entered the empty room. He saw the iron trunk lying open in one corner and no sign of any jewellery. He was shocked. He felt that this world had no purpose and that love and business were all useless. Phanibhushan did not even want to try to find out about his wife. He thought, she'd return if she wanted to. The old caretaker came and said, "What will come out of silence? You ought to find out about the lady of the house." So, he sent someone to Manimalika's father's house. He got the news that Mani had still not reached there.

At this everyone started searching for her. The police was informed, people on the riverside were asked but no information—either of the boat or the boatman—was received.

Losing all hope, Phanibhushan returned to his house. It was *Janmashtami* (Lord Krishna's birthday). It had been raining cats and dogs since morning. Phanibhushan had been sitting all alone. He looked at the things that Manimalika had collected over the years. He called out to her, "Come and light the lamp and wear your *sari*. Your things are waiting for you."

In the middle of the night, it stopped raining, but Phanibhushan continued sitting by the side of the window. Just then, he heard the sound of knocking and then, that of the jewellery. It seemed to be coming from the bank of the river. Phanibhushan was excited. He started looking out but could not see anything. The sound, however, continued to get closer. Then, right in front of the house, it stopped. The watchman had locked the gates and had gone to see the *Yatra*. Then the knocking became louder and stronger. Along with the sound of the jewellery, a loud hammer-like sound could also be heard. Phanibhushan could not contain himself any more.

Passing through the dark rooms, he climbed down the steps and came and stood before the locked gate. With both hands, he tried to shake the door open. The sound awoke him. He was surprised to see that he had sleep-walked to the gate. The sound of the jewellery had stopped but not the rain.

It was a dream but so close and true to life that Phanibhushan felt that just for a little, he had been deprived of the surprising success of his impossible desires.

The next day also, the *Yatra* was going on and the watchman was on leave. Phanibhushan ordered that the gates be left open. The watchman said, "Various people from various places come to see the fete. I don't feel confident about leaving the gates open." Phanibhushan did not agree. The watchman said, "In that case, I shall be present the whole night." Phanibhushan said, "There is no need. You can go and watch the *Yatra*." The watchman was amazed but he had to obey the orders.

The next day, Phanibhushan switched off the lamps and came and sat by the window. It was absolutely quiet. Just like the previous night, one could hear the sound of the thumping feet coming from the river bank, but Phanibhushan did not look that way. Although he longed to see yet he controlled himself with great effort.

The sound of jewels came in through the open door and was climbing up the spiral stairs. Phanibhushan could not suppress himself any more. His heart started pounding. The sound came close to the door of the room. It just needed to cross the door. Not being able to control himself any longer, Phanibhushan got up and screamed, "Mani!" And then, he woke up. There was none there. He beat his forehead.

The next day, the fete ended. Phanibhushan ordered that no one besides himself would stay at home that evening. He had fasted the whole day. In the evening, he sat by the window. The moon had still not risen. There was no boat there. Slowly, it became very dark. Even the stars could not be seen. His heart was at peace. He knew definitely that his thoughts would be proved right today; that death would reveal its mystery before him.

Like the previous night, the sound rose from the river side. Phanibhushan sat down in meditation. The sound came to his threshold, it rose over the spiral staircase, it crossed the huge verandah, and then stopped for a second, near the door of the bedroom.

Phanibhushan became anxious, but he did not open his eyes today. The sound entered the bedroom. It went near the place where the *sari* had been kept—folded, where the kerosene lamp stood, where the betel leaf was kept and then, finally, extremely close to Phanibhushan.

Phanibhushan then opened his eyes, rubbed them and in the light of the moon, saw a skeleton right in front of his stool! It had eight rings on eight fingers, bangles, armlets, necklaces and many other gold ornaments which were shining brightly. Her eyes seem exactly like the ones he had seen 18 years ago, on his wedding night. His blood froze. Those eyes were lifeless—a dead person's eyes.

The skeleton kept staring at Phanibhushan and then, raising the finger of her right hand, called him to follow her. Phanibhushan rose and started following the skeleton; down the spiral staircase, through the verandah, the entrance door, and out of the garden to the riverside. Then, it started climbing down into the river. Phanibhushan also followed suit. The moment his foot touched the water, he woke up. He did not see his guide before him. He shivered and his legs gave way. Phanibhushan fell into the stream. Although he knew how to swim, he did not feel like doing it. He again went into a deep slumber, after waking up for a little while.

The school master ended his story and waited for some time.

Suddenly, it was felt that except for him, everything else had become quiet.

I did not say anything for a long time and he too, could not see my expressions in the darkness. He asked me, "Did you not believe this story?"

I asked, "Do you believe it?"

He said, "No. I'll give you a few reasons why I don't believe it. Firstly, nature is not a writer of novels; she has a lot of work to do…"

I said, "Secondly, my name is Phanibhushan Saha."

The school master, without feeling even a little embarrassed, said, "In that case, I guessed right. What was your wife's name?"

I said, "Nrityakali."

20

THE BEGGAR WOMAN

I

THERE is a village in the huge mountain ranges of Kashmir. It has a number of small and dark huts. One can see a number of cows grazing in the green fields. The village belles were drawing water from the streams. The whole village seemed like a poet's dream.

A boy and a girl of the village really loved each other. They used to hold hands and play around the village, swimming and picking flowers together. In the afternoon, 16-year-old Amar Singh used to go and sit in the shade of a tree on the highest peak of the mountain and in a soft voice, recite the *Ramayana*. He used to burn with rage while reading the chapter of the kidnapping of Sita. Ten year-old Kamal Devi used to keep looking at him with her doe-like eyes and cry on hearing Sita's plight in the Ashok forest. They used to hold hands and return home in the evening when it got dark and the fireflies started flying about. Kamal Devi was a very proud girl. If anyone said anything rude to her, she'd hide her face on Amar Singh's chest and cry. She would stop only when Amar Singh consoled her. She had no one else except a widowed mother and the loving Amar Singh.

The girl's father was a very well-respected man of the village because he was a senior officer of the state. It was because she had been brought up in a rich family that Kamal never mixed around with the other girls of the village. She only played with Amar Singh, the son of Commander-in-Chief, Ajit Singh. Very recently, Kamal had got engaged to Amar Singh. Earlier, there had been a proposal from the son of a rich man named Mohanlal, but Kamal's father had refused saying that the boy's character was not good.

Then, Kamal's father died. Slowly, all the wealth and property was also lost, even their friends parted. The poor, orphaned widow gave up her house and started living in a small hut. She had to live in dire stress in poverty. How would her daughter be able to suffer the poverty? The loving mother had kept her daughter away from it till now.

Kamal was soon going to be married to Amar. Oblivious of the difficulties that her mother was going through, the two children would dream of a happy future, of their lives together and build castles in the air. Just then, news was received that war had broken out at the borders. Commander-in-chief Ajit Singh was to go to war and his son Amar Singh would also be going to train people for war.

In the evening, Amar said, "Kamal, I am leaving now. Who will you hear the *Ramayana* from?" The girl kept looking at him with eyes full of tears. "See Kamal, the sun will set again tomorrow, but I shall not come to knock at your door. And if...at the battlefield, I die..." Amar added.

Kamal embraced him and said, "But I love you Amar, why will you die?" Tears welled up in his eyes. He quickly wiped them and said, "Come, Kamal. It's getting dark. Let me escort you to your hut for the last time." They held hands and started walking towards their hut. The village belles were returning home singing and the stars started shining in the sky. When she went inside her house, she hugged her mother and wept bitterly, wondering why Amar was leaving her and going away. The same night, Amar left the village along with his father. After climbing up the last mountain, Amar looked back and saw his village. The thought of Kamal crying brought tears to his eyes. His father said, "What! A Rajput boy crying at the time of going to war?" Amar wiped his tears away.

It was winter. It had been snowing incessantly. A sad, poor girl was roaming around on the path of the mountains, with tears in her eyes. Her sick mother was lying without food, in the hut. The whole day, the girl had not been able to cook anything. She had not been able to build enough courage to beg for food either—in fact, she did not know how to ask for it or what to say! Slowly, it became very dark. The disappointed girl was returning to her hut. Weak, because she had not eaten, tired, because she had been walking; disappointed and hopeless, the girl could not walk. So, she lay down on the grass and went off to sleep. Her body felt senseless. She felt that she would be frozen under the snow. She folded her hands and remembering her mother, said, "O Goddess Bhagwati! Please don't kill me. Protect me; for if I die, my mother will cry—so will Amar!"

Slowly, the girl became unconscious. Not a soul passed that way. So, the girl kept lying between sheets of snow.

II

Kamal's sick mother was lying on the bed. A cold breeze was flowing fast into the hut. The old widow was shivering. Kamal had gone to beg and had still not returned. At every sound, her mother would sit up, thinking it was Kamal. She tried to get up many times, to go and look for Kamal, but she could not. Thinking that the worst might have happened to her, Kamal's mother cried and pleaded before God, "I am very unfortunate. Why could I not die? Even the girl, who has never known how to beg, has had to stand outside the house like an orphan! Poor girl! She is not used to walk long distances—how will she survive in this darkness, this snow, this rain?"

She was unable to get up. She could not see her daughter. The old woman started crying. One or two of her neighbours came. She held on to their feet and pleaded, "I don't know where my lost Kamal will be roaming around! Please go and find her." They said, "Sorry. We cannot go out in this darkness, snow and rain!"

She continued weeping, "Please go—just once! I am poor.

I don't have any money. What can I give you? The poor girl! She doesn't know the way. She has not even eaten anything today—bring her to her mother. God will bless you!" But, none heard her. Who would go out in this rain and thunder? Everyone went back into their houses.

Slowly, night came on. The widow had got tired, crying. She kept lying lifeless on her bed. Just then, she heard footsteps outside. Surprised, she kept looking at the door and in a weak voice, asked, "Have you come, Kamal?" Someone outside asked, "Who is at home?" Kamal's mother answered from inside. The man entered with a torch in his hand and said something to Kamal's mother. Hearing it, the mother screamed and fell down unconscious.

III

Kamal slowly regained consciousness. She opened her eyes and looked around. She saw that she was in a huge cave with dark, smoky clouds all around and piercing through them, were hard faces, glaring down at her. In fear, she closed her eyes and then, slowly, opened them again. One person asked her, "Who are you?"

In a frightened, shaking voice, she answered, "I am Kamal." She had thought that they would recognise her by her name only, but they did not.

Another person asked, "Why were you roaming around outside in such bad weather?"

The girl could not control herself any longer. She burst out crying and said, "My mother could not eat the whole day today."

All of them burst out laughing. Their laughter echoed in the cave. They seemed like robbers. She burst out crying with fear, "Please take me to my mother." They all laughed out aloud, once again. They questioned her about her place of residence, mother- father's name, etc. Finally, one person said, "We are bandits and you are our prisoner. We are sending a message to your mother that if she does not pay the required amount by the fixed time, we shall kill you."

Kamal cried and said, "Where will my mother get the money

from? She is extremely poor. She has no one else except me. Don't kill me. I have not done any harm to anybody." Again the robbers laughed loudly.

A messenger went to Kamal's mother. He went and said, "Your daughter has been made prisoner. I shall come three days from today. If you can give 500 gold coins, then we shall release her or else, your daughter will definitely be killed." Kamal's mother had fallen unconscious at hearing this only.

* * * *

Where would the poor widow find the money? She had already sold off all she had. However, she had kept aside a little jewellery to give to Kamal at the time of her wedding. Now, she sold them off too to bring her daughter back, yet it did not sum up to even one-fourth of their demand. There was nothing else she could sell off. She finally started going from door to door, begging for money. Even on the third day, she was not able to collect the amount demanded. Today the robber will come. If she is unable to give the money to him today, the one force that bound her to this world, would be torn apart!

* * * *

The frightened Kamal had drained herself crying. She thought that if her Amar Singh had been there, no such misfortune would had befallen.

The robbers would come and frighten her once in a while and she would cover her face with fright. However, there was one youth amongst the robbers who did not behave as cruelly as the others with Kamal. He would, lovingly, ask her many questions but Kamal could not answer any of them. He was the son of the robbers' chief. He had once asked her if she had any objection to marrying a robber. He even used to tempt her by saying that if Kamal married him, then he would protect her from death. After a day or two, Kamal saw that after having their drinks, the robbers were shining their knives.

* * * *

The robbers' messenger entered the widow's house and asked her where the money was? Whatever she had been able to collect from her begging, she put everything at his feet and said, "I have nothing else. All I had, I have given to you. Now, I beg you to please give my Kamal back to me."

The robber threw down the coins and shouted, "You will not get anything by telling lies. If you do not give the said amount, your daughter will definitely be killed today. I am going now. I shall tell the chief that he shall not get the amount decided; hence we should now begin our sacrificial prayers to Goddess Kali."

The widow begged, cried but could not melt the robber's stone heart. When the robber was about to go, she said, "Please do not go yet. Wait a little longer. Let me try once more." And, she went out.

IV

A proposal had come earlier for Kamal to get married to Mohanlal. Because it did not happen, Mohanlal was a little angry and upset. He had heard the entire incident related to Kamal and so he had immediately sent for the family priest to fix an auspicious day for the wedding.

There was no one as wealthy as Mohanlal in the village. The troubled widow finally came to his house. Mohan sniggered and said, "What a great thing! How have you come to this poor man's house after so many days?"

The widow said, "Do not make fun. I am poor and have come to you for alms."

"Why? What has happened?" asked Mohan.

The widow told him the entire story.

Mohan asked, "In that case, what do I have to do?"

Widow – "You'll have to save Kamal's life."

Mohan – "Why? Is Amar Singh not here?"

The widow understood the taunt. She said, "Even if I had to move from forest to forest in the absence of a place to live, even if I had died of hunger, I would not had requested you for even a grain; but, today I am in a great problem. If you do not fulfil this request of this widow, then your heartlessness will be remembered forever."

Mohan – "Let me tell you one thing. Kamal is not bad to look at. It's not that I did not like her. I do not see any other objection to my marrying her. I shall not hide anything from you. I am not in a position to give alms without a reason."

Widow – "But her marriage has already been fixed with Amar."

Mohan did not give any reply. He opened his Accounts Book and started calculating something—as if there was no one in the room. Time was passing. She was not sure whether the robber was still at home or not. The widow cried and said, "Don't trouble me any more, Mohan! Time is passing!"

Mohan asked her to wait while he finished his work.

Finally, if the widow had not agreed to the marriage proposal, then it was doubtful if the work would have been finished the whole day or not. The widow took the money from Mohanlal, gave it to the dacoit and he went away.

The same day, the girl returned to her mother.

Thus, the orphan girl was forced to marry Mohanlal.

* * * *

Many years have passed...the war has ended...the soldiers have come back home. The widow heard that Ajit Singh had been killed and Amar, imprisoned; but she did not give this news to her daughter. The girl was married to Mohanlal.

Mohanlal's anger had not subsided. His vengeful nature was not satisfied by marrying. He used to torture the poor, helpless girl. She was in great pain, but the poor girl could not even cry.

She'd wipe off her tears for fear of being scolded by Mohanlal.

V

The rays of the morning sun decorated the snow-capped mountain peaks. The sleeping widow woke up to the sound of knocking at the door. She opened the door and saw Amar Singh standing before her in a soldier's uniform.

Quickly, Amar asked, "Kamal, where is Kamal?" He heard that she was in her husband's house. For a moment, he was shocked. What all he had thought! He had thought that he was returning home after a long time, that after the mad shaking of the war, he was returning home to sleep in the peace of matrimony. He had thought that when he'd go and stand at the gate, Kamal would come running to him and embrace him. They'd go up to the peak of the mountain where they had spent most of their childhood and narrate stories of the war to her. Now, it seemed as if lightening had fallen on his dreams. But, although his heart was in turmoil, he did not show any sign of it.

Mohan left Kamal at her mother's house and went out for work. Kamal was now 15 years old. She wanted to string a garland in the garden one day and another day, brought out her childhood toys, but was unable to do either because she had thought that if Amar comes back, they'll both play together and string garlands together. Sometimes, Kamal used to feel miserable at the thought of how long she had not seen Amar. Sometimes, she would go on top of the same mountain peak where she had spent her childhood, plying and blankly staring at the stars.

Mohan had been greatly upset and angry because Kamal used to weep for Amar and for her mother and while sending her to her mother's home he would think, "Let her suffer the shortage and scarcity a little; after that I'll see who cries for whom!" Kamal used to cry secretly at her mother's house. Her mother had never got to know about it.

One day, Kamal heard that her Amar had returned home. She remembered his childhood face and in pain, she went out of the house, especially to meet Amar.

Amar was sitting on the peak of the same mountain and remembering each and every episode of their childhood and comparing his bright childhood to the dark desert of his future life—without friends, without help, without refuge, with no one to call and ask him, none to show sympathy, he'd roam around alone.

Slowly, the sound from the village stopped. All Amar could hear was the sound of the wind blowing. Suddenly he heard someone calling out to him. He turned around and saw Kamal. In a moment, she came close to him, embraced him and putting her head on his shoulder, called his name out again. Amar too, cried. Then, suddenly, he moved away. Kamal said many things to him of which he answered a few. And then, she went away, crying.

****

Kamal had thought that her childhood friend Amar had returned and that she was the Kamal of her childhood and that they'd begin playing once again from the next day. Although Amar had been badly hurt by her yet, he did not get angry with her. However, just so that it wouldn't disturb Kamal's married life, he went away somewhere—nobody knew where!

The young girl's heart broke. The proud girl had thought of him all these days; she had gone running to meet her childhood friend, why then did Amar ignore her? She could not understand anything. One day, she had asked her mother that. Mother had told her that there was nothing surprising in the fact that Commander-in-Chief Amar Singh, who had spent some years in the big houses of the palace, should forget a poor girl. This pierced the poor girl's heart deeply. She was not upset that Amar Singh's had behaved rudely with her.

The unfortunate girl used to think that she was poor, she had nothing, she was senseless and not fit for him—then what right did she have, to love him? How could she, the poor Kamal, expect him to love her?

She spent the whole night crying. She never expressed her sorrow before anyone, but slowly, the sorrow started taking its toll. She wouldn't talk to anyone; she'd sit quietly and contemplate the whole day and the whole night. She stopped laughing and crying. Slowly, she started losing weight and could not get up. Despite a lot of effort, the widow, her mother, could not understand the reason for the child's sorrow and therefore, could not find a cure for her disease. Kamal could herself understand that she was moving towards death. She had no desires. She only prayed to God that she could see Amar at the time of her death.

Kamal's pain became more intense. She started fainting. Her mother and her village friends were all standing around. The widow did not have so much money that she could take on the burden of her medical expenses. Mohan was not around and even if he was, nothing could be expected from him. She would work day and night to look after Kamal. After a lot of begging and pleading, she was able to convince one doctor to come and examine Kamal.

It was raining heavily. The people on the mountains had not witnessed this kind of a rain and storm for many years. The beggar woman gave up hope that the doctor would come to examine Kamal. She kept staring at Kamal's face. Once, Kamal regained consciousness and stared at her mother. After many days, tears were seen in Kamal's eyes. The widow also started crying.

Suddenly, the sound of horse's hoofs was heard. The widow rose, thinking that the doctor had come. The door opened and the doctor walked in. Drops of water were falling from his clothes. He went and stood before the girl's bed. The girl looked up at his face. It was not the doctor—but the serious Amar Singh. The troubled girl kept staring at his face; tears fell down her large eyes and a laughter brightened Kamal's face. But, she could not tolerate so much joy. Slowly, her eyes closed, her heartbeats stopped and the light went out. The girls put flowers over her. Amar ran out, broken hearted.

From that day onwards, the widow became mad and would go around begging and every evening, sit in her hut and cry.

□□□